# ALSO BY ALLISON BETTES

**Cupid Meets Crime Scene Series**

RED FLAG WARNING

ROGUE WAVE

ZERO VISIBILITY

* * *

**The Ranger Shield Security Series**

BETRAYAL & NEW BEGINNINGS

INSTINCT & NEW IDENTITY

DECEPTION & NEW DIRECTION

RESTART & NEW REVENGE

* * *

**The Raising the Bar Series**

*A Ranger Shield Security Spin-Off Series*

NEW ROOTS

NEW RULES

* * *

For more information visit www.AllisonBettes.com.

# HEAT ADVISORY

CUPID MEETS CRIME SCENE BOOK TWO

## ALLISON BETTES

This is a work of fiction created without use of AI technology. Any names, characters, businesses, places, events, and incidents portrayed in this novel are either products of the author's imagination or are used fictitiously. Any resemblance to actual persons, living or dead, places, or events is purely coincidental or fictional.

**HEAT ADVISORY**
**Cupid Meets Crime Scene, Book 2**
**First edition.**
**© 2026 Allison Bettes, LLC**
**All rights reserved.**
Cover Design © 2026 by KJaspersenDesigns
Available in ebook and print.



www.allisonbettes.com

# DEDICATION

*For anyone who's ever had a bad first date...or second...or third—and the questionable decisions that followed* 😊

# HEAT ADVISORY

# 1

—*It's science*

## Cora

Have you ever had a kiss that was so incredibly good, it ruined you for all other men?

For me, that was my high school crush, Jay Rainer.

He was the epitome of handsome, everything my teenage brain had imagined. That first kiss didn't disappoint—it sailed past the usual cliches of stars and butterflies and landed somewhere deeper. He made me feel special. Noticed. Like I actually mattered to him.

The only problem was he left two days after that kiss, never to speak to me again.

What was worse, his sister, Morgan, was my best friend, so I still heard everything about him through her, which only dug the knife in deeper. Just like I filled her in on what was happening with all my sisters, she did the same about her brother.

It wasn't her fault. Morgan didn't know that her brother and I had kissed. So how would she know that every time she brought him up, it was both information I craved and loathed at the same time?

Jay had left town right after graduating because he was drafted to play for a minor league baseball team in Texas. He played for them for two years, and just before he got his big break, he suffered an ulnar collateral ligament tear and had Tommy John surgery.

I still remember getting Morgan's call that he was in the hospital having surgery. I swear that phone call took years off my life.

*"The surgery went well, but the doctor said the damage was worse than they originally thought," she said.*

*"What does that mean?" I asked.*

*She sighed, and I felt the weight of that sigh deep inside me.*

*"It means his baseball career is over."*

*My heart tightened like a vise was gripped around it. This was Jay's dream, and it was over before it ever really had a chance to take off.*

*"Can't he do physical therapy or something? Maybe see if another doctor can do something else?"*

*There had to be something that someone could do.*

*"I don't know." Her voice showed that she was just as sad as I was for her brother.*

After his baseball career ended, he stayed in Texas but moved on to his next dream—becoming a firefighter.

Not long after, she mentioned that the heat had gotten

to him, so he'd moved north to become a firefighter in Colorado. She missed him and wished he would move back home, but she thought he was embarrassed because of how his career had turned out. Especially because their dad pushed the major league dream so hard.

So, color me shocked when I was in Las Vegas at a training exercise and saw Jay across the room.

The same man who, even years later, still occupied an enormous amount of space in my mind.

My sister Iris's voice cut into my thoughts. "What do you keep staring at?"

"Umm...nothing," I lied to her, shaking my head to help clear my brain. "Did you get that thing to load yet?"

My sister was a meteorologist with the National Weather Service in Las Vegas, and I was the Nevada State Hydrologist, and we were here to do a fire and flood safety training event.

"Yeah, it just took a little magic, sweet talk, and a full reset of the program," Iris's coworker Christine responded. "PowerPoint is up and running—finally."

The event included the three of us, plus some local firefighters, the fire marshal, EMTs, the Public Works Department, Nevada Highway Patrol, a public information officer from the Las Vegas PD, emergency managers, and a few local TV meteorologists. It was a large group to make sure everything went smoothly in an emergency—prepare for the worst but hope for the best.

My hope, however, was dwindling that the man across

the large conference room was just a Jay lookalike when he finally looked my way and our eyes connected.

*Okay, be cool. He's looking at you. Do not look nervous. Maybe he won't recognize you.*

That prayer went right out the window as he smiled and began walking my way.

"Oh, no," I mumbled.

"What's wrong?" Iris asked as she looked up to follow where my gaze was aimed. "Do you know that guy walking toward us?"

She mumbled that last part under her breath so only the three of us at our table could hear it.

"Who are we looking at?" Christine said, causing me to close my eyes and hope that this was just a dream I would wake up from.

"Hey, Cora," the smooth, masculine voice said.

I opened my eyes to see him smiling at me, but no words came out of my mouth.

*Cora, you're an adult. Act like it.*

At my lack of response, his attention turned to my sister. "Hey, Iris. Jay Rainer. We went to high school together."

"Oh yes, Jay!" Iris exclaimed, nodding as she realized that she remembered him. "You were voted 'most likely to become famous'."

"Yeah, well, I have some disappointing news regarding that," he replied with a somber tone but a smirk on his face.

"Oh, it's okay," Iris replied and pointed to me. "People

voted Cora 'most likely to own and operate the Scholastic book fair,' and that never came true either."

It was true. I was a book nerd in school. When I wasn't studying, tutoring someone, or helping out on the family farm, I was at the library. It was my sanctuary. My escape.

"I think Morgan might have mentioned that," Jay said, a small grin tugging at his mouth—a mouth that was just as sexy as the rest of his body. "It's good to see you both."

He'd always had an athletic build, but he looked even more handsome now. He had short brown hair that was practically buzzed on the sides, sun-kissed skin, and muscles upon muscles built into his tall frame. He also had stunning whiskey-colored eyes—eyes that were darkly romantic and boring into me.

*Was it getting hot in here? It felt like it.*

It was hotter than hell outside, so maybe the air conditioner had stopped working. That must be why I was sweating in places I had no right to be sweating.

"So, you both live in Vegas now?" he asked, but before I could respond, Iris chimed in first.

"I do, but Cora lives up near Reno. She travels all over the state for her job, so she's here for this event. You live here too?"

His eyes flared with something so fast I couldn't decipher what it was, but then just as quickly, they went back to normal. If I hadn't been staring at him, I likely would have missed it.

"I'm actually up in the Reno area as well," he responded, a growing smile taking over his face. "Just took a job there. This event helps me complete my fire investigator certification."

There was a lot to break down there, but I focused on one thing.

*He lives in Reno now? Why hadn't Morgan told me?*

"Oh, my gosh. That's so cool," Iris said, excitedly clapping her hands. "You and Cora should get lunch sometime."

*Oh. My. God. She did not just say that.*

He stared at me for a second, his gaze burning a hole through me with its intensity. I knew there was no way my face was not turning fifty shades of pink.

"I'd actually like that," he said to me as mischief lit his eyes. "I just moved there earlier this year, so I haven't quite learned my way around. I'd love a tour guide."

"Um...I'm not sure I would...umm...have the time," I told him, stuttering my way through this bullshit made-up excuse.

"You just said you have next week off, so you should show him around," Iris said, smiling slyly at me.

*Oh my God. I was going to kill her later.*

"Great," Jay said excitedly. "Let me get your phone number so we can connect."

He pulled his phone out to type my number into it.

*Oh my God. He asked for my phone number. Breathe. Normal breathing.*

I did my best to look casual as I rattled off my phone number and he typed it in.

"Perfect. I'll send you a text so you have my number

too," he said to me. "I'll let you go since I'm sure you ladies are busy. Good to see you both."

"You too, Jay," Iris said gleefully.

"Oh, I'm sorry. I forgot to introduce myself," he said to Christine, holding out his hand. "I'm Jay Rainer."

"Nice to meet you," she responded as she shook his hand.

"Same," he replied and then turned to Iris and me. "It was good to see you, ladies."

I silently waved, like a moron, with a loopy grin on my face.

*There went the last of my dignity and grace.*

"We're all going to go out to dinner when this is over, if you'd like to join us," Iris offered.

Before I could even think of a response, Jay smiled and responded.

"I wish I could, but unfortunately, there was a big fire on the south side of town that appears to be arson," he said solemnly. "I need to hop on a flight and get back as soon as this is over so our team can get out there and dive into the investigation."

I'd heard about that suspected arson. The fire had been bad. If it was arson, I hope they would be able to find who did it before another one was set.

"Thank you for the offer. I'll see you next week," he said to me and winked.

*He winked. Winked.*

My high school crush. The man I had thought about

so many times, in many inappropriate ways, had just winked at me.

*Why was it suddenly hard to get a full breath of air?*

I blankly stared at him as he walked away, retreating to his original place on the other side of the room.

Then my view was blocked by my sister waving her hand in front of my face. "Yoo-hoo. Earth to Cora."

I turned to my sister and angrily whispered to her, "Why would you tell him I could show him around?"

"Because you had the biggest crush on him in high school, and as your sister and pseudo wingman…or woman, I'm here to help you," Iris explained.

I turned to Christine, who was just watching us go back and forth. "Is murder illegal in *all* fifty states? Asking for a friend."

She snorted and chuckled at my question. "I think he's cute, and you should definitely meet up with him."

Ugh. Now they were ganging up on me.

It's not that I was unhappy to see him. He was my biggest crush ever—of course I was excited to see him. I just didn't like surprises or being caught off guard.

I was a planner. I liked being able to create a plan B, C, and D in my head.

Jay appearing out of nowhere had me feeling completely off balance. I did not like being unprepared for variables I had not accounted for.

"You don't want to murder me," Iris said. "In fact, you'll probably be thanking me later, so I will go ahead and just tell you you're welcome right now. However, if he hurts you or treats you bad, then I will personally help you bury the body."

I rolled my eyes at her just as my phone buzzed with an incoming text. I looked down to see a new message from a new number.

UNKNOWN NUMBER:

This is Jay. I'm looking forward to our date next week. ;)

*Date?*

Jay—the sexiest man I had ever met, and the one I'd had the biggest crush on since I was a teenager—just wrote that he was looking forward to a date...with me.

*Oh, God.*

Expect the unexpected.

That was what I was learning from Jay Rainer. And I didn't like it one bit.

# 2

**"The moment you sit down, someone will ask you for something. That likelihood increases exponentially if there is a child anywhere nearby."**
—*It's science*

## Cora

*Twelve Years Ago*

I was staying over at my best friend Morgan's house for what was likely our 490th sleepover. I practically lived there when I wasn't in my own home, and I loved being there. Her mom and dad were like second parents to me —the good kind that I wish my own biological parents had been.

I was born Cora Marie Carson to a seemingly loving couple just outside San Diego. A few years later, my sister Hazel was born, and we were the perfect little family—

until we weren't. Our father, Craig Carson, was a good dad, but he liked to gamble. He was always into get-rich-quick schemes, and after a while, our mom finally gave up on him. She left, and she did so without taking Hazel and me with her.

Dad tried to take care of us. He loved us in his own way, and he tried to be a caring dad, but it was a struggle. He either couldn't or didn't want to hold down a steady job, so he went back to gambling. Unfortunately, he gambled with the wrong people and lost and then got himself nearly killed and put in prison.

Hazel and I were put into foster care, but since the police were concerned my dad's enemies might come after us for collateral, we were moved to the northern part of the state and put into the custody of Winnie and Tia O'Hara. Winnie and Tia were sisters who had also grown up in the foster system, constantly bumping around because no one wanted two older sisters.

They had dedicated their adult lives to opening their doors to as many foster girls as they could, determined to give them stability instead of endless moves. Some girls hadn't stayed long, usually because a parent or relative eventually stepped in to care for them. But for the ones whose families either couldn't—or simply wouldn't—take them back, the O'Haras made sure we always had a place to belong. Hazel and I were two of those lucky ones.

Winnie—who we just called Mom—and Tia—which was Spanish for aunt, so we'd always called her Auntie—

lived on a small property in Stratus Cove, a coastal town in Northern California. The place was beautiful—lush green landscape, salty ocean air, and friendly people who waved at you on the street. Being a small town, everybody knew everybody's business, but that also meant they knew what the O'Hara women did. Nobody batted an eyelash when another foster kid appeared at their house. It was just accepted.

I had lucked out, not only with the O'Haras, but also with Morgan's family as well, which was why I enjoyed coming over here so often.

Morgan was sprawled across her bed, flipping through her CDs while we talked about our school dance like it was some kind of natural disaster that we desperately wanted to be a part of.

The homecoming dance. The words alone made my stomach tighten.

I really wanted Morgan's brother to ask me, but I knew that would never happen. He was a senior, and I was a junior, and while we'd gotten close the last few months as I tutored him, I knew he only saw me as his little sister's best friend and nothing more.

"My only option is Garrison, and I think that's only because Becky told him I was a slut," Morgan said. "I thought about going with him, getting pictures, dancing, and then telling him I wasn't feeling good and having my loser brother just pick me up, but that's too complicated."

"Well, we can go together, then," I told her.

"Wait...I thought you said that guy from the debate team asked you...What was his name?"

"Chadwick," I replied. "And no. I don't even know him.

"He's kind of a nerd, though," Morgan said.

"Yeah, well, so am I." I shrugged because it was the truth.

I wasn't embarrassed by it. It was who I was. I was a self-proclaimed bookworm and loved school—especially science and math.

"I wish we had better options at our school," Morgan whined. "The cute ones are jerks, the ugly ones don't want to go to the dance, and the few in between who are left don't notice us."

Outside of each other, Morgan and I didn't hang out with many people. Unfortunately, this meant not a lot of people knew us.

"Yeah, well, we're kind of invisible to most people," I told her, not that she didn't already know it. "I'm pretty sure most of the guys don't even think of us as an option."

Morgan opened her mouth like she was about to argue, but my stomach growled before she could, loud enough to derail the moment.

"Snack time!" Morgan said, switching gears to the new topic at hand. "Will you go get the snacks? I'll get us some new jams to listen to."

I had just sat down and was nice and relaxed, but I got up and made my way into the hallway as Morgan turned up the stereo. I almost ran straight into Jay, who was just a few feet away from the door, his expression so serious, it made me stop short.

"There's no way you could ever be invisible, Cora," he said quietly, or maybe it just seemed quiet compared to Morgan's music. "You're too pretty and smart for that to happen."

I froze.

*Did he just say that?*

For a second, it felt like my heart forgot how to beat, and clearly my brain did too, because I couldn't even muster a thank you. I just stared at him. He smiled, like he knew exactly what he'd done to me, winked, and then walked away like he hadn't just shattered my entire sense of reality.

It was winter break, and we were out of school for a full two and a half weeks for the holidays. It was five days before Christmas, and Morgan and I were having a sleepover before her family left in two days to go visit their grandparents who lived up in Oregon.

We had just settled in to the living room to watch a movie with all our snacks when Jay walked in.

"What are you two up to?" He was leaning against the doorframe with a big grin on his face. God, he looked so good standing there in a pair of gray sweatpants and a long-sleeved white tee. The tee was tighter around his upper arms where his muscles were, and I felt myself getting warmer just picturing what those muscles would feel like if they were wrapped around me, holding me tight.

"We're watching a chick flick, so go away," Morgan responded.

"I thought we were watching the new James Bond movie?" I asked her, confused because we had just talked about it.

"Ooh, I'll watch the Bond movie," Jay said and then began to walk into the living room toward the couch where I was sitting.

Morgan sighed dramatically. "I didn't want him watching with us." Though she grumbled the words quietly, Jay must have still heard her.

"Too late," he said, taking a seat to the right of me on the couch.

It was a small couch and only fit the two of us. Morgan was to my left in the recliner with the side table between us, filled with snacks and drinks.

"If you talk during the movie or ruin it in any way, then you're getting kicked out," Morgan threatened.

Jay used his fingers to zip across his lips—giving the universal signal for "my lips are sealed." While Morgan grumbled a bit more, she let it go and began to use the remote to cue up the movie.

I, however, looked over at Jay after having felt his gaze directly on me. As soon as our eyes made contact, he gave me a small smile and shot me a sly look.

*What was that for?*

The three of us watched the movie intensely, all keyed into the action scenes, at least until the last twenty minutes…when Morgan promptly fell asleep.

"I have no idea how she can fall asleep during the best part of movies," Jay whispered, leaning into me. He was so close I could smell his Axe body spray.

*Why was he wearing Axe body spray before bed?*

"I don't know, but she does it all the time," I replied with a smile.

"She's done it for as long as I can remember," Jay added.

We finished watching the movie, and then Jay leaned over me, his left arm behind me as he grabbed onto the back of the couch, his right arm reaching over to grab the remote from the side table.

He could have just asked me to hand him the remote. Instead, he put his body in front of mine and seemed to take his time returning to his position next to me.

I didn't mind, though. I got an up close and personal look at his face, broad shoulders, and hair. Oh, how I wished so badly I could run my fingers through it.

He changed the channel from the movie and switched it to ESPN. I took that as my cue to wake Morgan up and head up to her room for sleep, even though I wasn't really tired yet.

Just as I started to rise, Jay put his hand on my thigh. It was a soft touch, but the tingles that radiated on my leg were intense. I had pink plaid flannel pajama bottoms on, and I could still feel the heat on my skin from his palm.

"You don't need to leave," he whispered. "We can watch another movie or something if you don't want to watch sports."

I really wanted to stay. To be close to him. But it also felt weird with Morgan sitting next to us, even if she was asleep.

"Umm…"

"Chill for a bit. It's not even eleven o'clock," he said, his hand still resting on my thigh, practically burning a hole through my skin. "I'll help you carry her up later."

"Okay." My mouth responded for me since my brain was currently freaking out and in panic mode.

He winked back at me. Again.

A tic. It had to be some kind of tic. That's why he winked at me so often.

Ultimately, we never ended up watching another movie. We sat there and quietly talked about the movie we'd just watched, which transitioned into our favorite action movies and then our favorite movies in general.

We chatted together for over an hour about a variety of things. It was shortly after midnight when Jay made a comment about one of his teammates accidentally dropping a weight on his foot because he was trying to show off to some girl who walked by. I laughed, which in turn woke Morgan up.

There were more than half a dozen other sleepovers I had at Morgan's house over the next few months where Jay joined us for a movie night. Some of them really were chick flicks, and I was surprised to find he watched them with us. More importantly, after each one of them, Jay and I stayed up to talk together after Morgan had fallen asleep—right on cue—during the best part of the movie.

I found myself convincing Morgan more and more to watch movies every time I stayed at her house, just in the hope that Jay might join us.

# 3

**"Storm chasing is just extreme dating
for weather nerds."**
—*It's science*

## Jay

I still couldn't believe Cora had been at that event in Las Vegas. The same one I'd been at.

In hindsight, I should have known, given her job and the event being filled with emergency management and planners, but I had been so focused on my job that I had almost missed her.

Almost.

Though not because she was someone you could miss. She had always been on the slightly taller side. My guess was she was close to five foot seven or eight. Her long dark hair had been pulled back into a ponytail, but all that did was highlight those gorgeous teal eyes. I'd spent many hours as a teenager staring into those eyes and even more hours dreaming about them.

I had intended to reach out to Cora right away after I got back to Reno, but I'd learned she was sticking around an extra day in Vegas with her sister, so I held off. Two days seemed long enough to let her get settled back home, but not too long for her to think I had forgotten about her.

Plus, I didn't *want* to wait too long. I had waited years to get Cora to go on a date with me—officially—and I wanted to take advantage of this opportunity.

In high school, there had been two things I thought about constantly. Two things I wanted most in my young teenage life. The first was to become a professional baseball player. The second was my sister's best friend—Cora.

However, everything seemed to have gotten in the way. Not just years ago, but even now.

As soon as I returned, I was thrown into the fire—literally. I had gotten the call from Hal Thompson—my future boss if I secured this fire investigator role I really wanted—who requested I shadow this particular fire inspection.

Two people had died in a fire a few days ago, and it was looking more and more like another fire from earlier this month, under suspiciously similar circumstances. That meant they wanted all hands on deck—even people like me—for the investigation.

For me, being able to observe and train on a real case was crucial. I went along with the crew as they assessed the scene and learned the ropes. It was exactly what I had wanted to do, and it looked great to my boss. The only downfall: I was delayed in reaching out to Cora.

I arrived to find Thompson and a few others already there, including Trent. He worked with me at Station 12 often on the same shift as me, so we were part of the same family. He'd been great, up until he learned we were both applying for the inspector job. We were still civil, but there was definitely tension when it came to the job opening.

"Rainer, thanks for joining us on your day off," Thompson greeted me. "I'll have you both follow the BAER team and assist where you can."

He assigned Trent to follow a man named Bernard, and I was to follow Darren.

We worked side by side with Burned Area Emergency Response—or BAER—on these cases, so I was looking forward to getting some hands-on experience. Bernard was the team leader, and I was hoping to follow him since he had two decades of experience, but I was happy for the opportunity period, so I would go with my guy and learn what I could.

Darren was on the taller side, maybe an inch or so shorter than me, but he was definitely skinnier and lacked any real muscle mass. He had black hair that was fully styled with way too much gel for investigating in the woods. He was lucky the fires were out, or his hair would be one of the first things to go with all those flammable products in it.

This particular fire had been on the northern side of a state forest, which meant protected land that was hard to get to. In theory, that should limit our available suspects, but I'd learned over the years that crazy people would go to extremes to set these fires. The fire had spread quickly thanks to all the dry brush, but since there were no homes or businesses on park property, there was no structural damage.

After following Darren and his crew around for over an hour, I was convinced he was an egotistical idiot. He'd only started a few months ago but acted like he ran the department.

"I'll have you know that dry trees burn faster than moist ones," Darren had informed us.

*No shit, Captain Obvious.*

It was why we always did safety lessons on our station's social media page about keeping Christmas trees well-watered. A dry, neglected Christmas tree could go up in flames in just ten seconds.

He knew a lot about the forest and fires, but his cocky bedside manner could use some work.

I'd noticed a few others on his team occasionally rolling their eyes, so at least I wasn't the only one.

At the end, I'd met back up with Trent while we waited for Thompson.

"What was Bernard like?" I asked, curious how he compared to Darren.

"Fine." Trent shrugged his shoulders, sounding bored. "He's no more qualified than we are for this gig, so I just followed along and smiled at everything he said and pretended to care. He's old, so hopefully he'll be out soon and I can take over."

I fought the groan that I really wanted to release.

*Jesus. From one egotistical asshole to another.*

The biggest takeaways were that the fires were definitely arson, and whoever was setting them was growing more confident, increasing both in frequency and aggression.

That evening, I finally had the time to message Cora. After an exhausting day, this was just the medicine I needed.

ME:

If you're not busy, would you like to grab breakfast on Monday? I could also use some help to pick out whatever ugly penguin suit my sister has insisted I wear to her wedding.

CORA:

You haven't tried on your tux yet? It's less than a month away!

Of course, that was the part she would focus on.

ME:

Not yet. So, is that a yes to breakfast, and then you'll go with me to help me figure out what to wear?

I saw the dots pop up and then disappear once and then a second time. Shit. Maybe I shouldn't have mentioned the suit. Just food.

CORA:

Sure. How about I meet you at the café
across the street from the bridal store at
eight?

ME:

I'll pick you up so we can save gas.

CORA:

I have some things to do later that day,
so I will just meet you there.

I had hoped to pick her up, find out where she lived, and treat this like a real date—and hopefully try to drag it out and spend the whole rest of the day with her, but maybe she had other plans after that.

ME:

That sounds great. I'm looking forward
to our date ;)

There. Hopefully, that cleared it up for her.

Because this was a date. At least to me, it was. And hopefully it all went well enough that we had more dates after.

If Cora only knew how much I had thought about her over the past few years, she would probably think I was a stalker.

If she only knew I'd picked Reno because Morgan told me she lived here. I'd had two job offers—Sacramento and here—but the second I realized we could be in the same city again, the choice made itself. Knowing Cora was building a life here made the move feel less like a gamble and more like a second chance at something I'd never quite let go of.

Morgan had been bugging me to move back home to California, but I just couldn't do it. I couldn't be that close to people I grew up with and see the sympathy in their eyes when it came to my baseball career. Most importantly, I couldn't face my dad. Morgan told me he didn't care, but it had been his dream for me to go pro. Being a great baseball player had been my identity for so long that after my career ended, I struggled to find myself.

Firefighting gave me purpose. That job felt more like what I was *meant* to do, rather than just simply what I was good at.

I took my first job as a firefighter in southeast Texas, and while I'd loved the job, I hated the heat—despised it actually. So I'd transferred to Colorado. I'd enjoyed that job too, and it was definitely busier because there were a lot more forest fires than in Texas, but it still didn't feel right.

I had been texting with Morgan one day, and she mentioned she was going to Reno to visit Cora because she had just moved there to take her dream job. Reno wasn't far from where we had grown up. Only about a five-hour drive from our coastal California town. That would put me closer to family, but not so close that they would come to visit me often. Most importantly, it would put me right next to Cora.

The woman I had dreamed about since high school.

Logically, it made no sense. In fact, it was kind of

ridiculous, really. I was a thirty-year-old man, yet my brain kept replaying our kiss, our tutoring sessions, and late-night movies over and over again in my head—a loop of nostalgic moments.

Now, years later, I found myself often wondering if my mild obsession with her was simply because we never got to finish what we started, or if it was something deeper. Was it because of the way she used to look at me like I was the only person in the room, and she cared, not just because I was a good baseball player?

I knew I was attracted to her—that was never in question. But I found other women attractive too. They just never had the extra wow factor like Cora had—the thing that drew me in and captivated me like she had.

Maybe the universe was giving me a second chance to get the timing right and give this thing a go and see if it was more than just a high school crush.

"Hey sis," I said, answering the phone after I saw she was calling.

"Have you ordered your tux in the style I sent you yet?" she practically whined into the phone as she reminded me I needed to order my groomsman's attire.

"I was planning to do that today," I responded.

"You are such a terrible liar," she shot back, and I could sense her rolling her eyes at me through the phone.

"Remind me who all is in your bridesmaid and groomsmen group thing?" Hopefully someone else I knew was in there and I could get some details on where to get this penguin suit, since I had no idea where I'd put the information she sent me.

"They're called a bridal party, and Lewis's brother, Pete, is going to be his best man. You're a groomsman. Laura, Lewis's twin sister, is my bridesmaid, and Cora is my maid of honor." I was half listening as she listed off her names but stopped at the mention of Cora.

Logically, I knew she would be a part of the wedding, but still, hearing her name made me smile.

This would give me the perfect excuse to keep texting her about all things wedding related.

"Also, you haven't responded about whether you are bringing a plus one to the wedding or not," she grumbled.

"No, I'm not. I want to be able to focus on my groomsman duties and help out with anything the rest of the *bridal party* might need." That was a half-truth.

Even before I knew that Cora was going to be in the wedding, I knew she would definitely be attending since she was Morgan's best friend. My original plan was to use that event to make my first approach in trying to secure a second chance with her. I hadn't realized fate would intervene and bring us together for the event in Las Vegas weeks before.

Hopefully, we would have met up a few times—or maybe a dozen—before that, so maybe I could convince her to be my unofficial plus one. Everything was finally coming together for my timeline to make Cora mine.

She sighed almost in relief. "Thank God."

"What does that mean?" I asked, almost offended.

"Dude, I don't know about your personal life lately, mostly because I don't care who you date, but you had some serious bimbos attached to your arm whenever you had big events when you played ball in Texas. I know they supposedly grow 'em big in Texas, but those women took that to heart with their big hair, big boobs, and big attitudes with delusions of grandeur."

She was right, but there was part of me that still felt I had to defend myself and reputation, which was the only reason I let slip from my mouth what I did. "I'll have you know the only woman I am meeting up with anytime soon is actually Cora."

My eyes closed as soon as I said it. I winced as I heard her shocked gasp follow.

"Cora? As in *my* Cora?" Her voice was a mix of hope, excitement, and then confusion. "Why?"

I wasn't ready to tell her my plans about getting Cora to go out on a date with me just yet, so I gave her a half-truth for now. "She's going with me to pick out my suit on Monday. I figured since she's been helping you plan this whole thing, she could help me out, too."

"Oh, that's actually a good idea." I heard Morgan's relieved sigh, which was a bit of a blow to my confidence that she didn't think I could handle picking out something as simple as a suit. "Plus, it's a tux, not a suit. This is a formal wedding, bro."

"That's what I meant," I told her.

She chuckled back. "Sure. So…" she said slowly. "Should I be worried?"

"About what?" I feigned ignorance.

"You suddenly caring deeply about formalwear—and my best friend." The sarcasm was apparent in her voice, which only made me want to tease her more.

I smiled to myself. "I care about all the things you care about too—it's what makes me the world's greatest brother."

"Uh-huh." The sarcasm was clear in her voice. "Just remember. This is my wedding."

"I know that."

"And Cora is my maid of honor."

"Also know that, too."

"And if you do anything stupid, like kiss her or break her heart—"

If she only knew.

"Morgan…again…greatest brother in the world here. You don't have to worry."

"Famous last words," she grumbled under her breath, but I could also hear the smile in her voice.

After teasing her a little more, we hung up. I found myself smiling just thinking about meeting up with Cora. Just saying her name out loud felt like stepping into something real—something I hadn't let myself have for years.

I knew deep down I wasn't just trying to win her over. I was trying to become someone worthy of her. Her support for me, even back when we were in high school, was front sand center in my thoughts.

After baseball, I'd seen a therapist. Another teammate had recommended the guy. He specialized in professional athletes whose careers ended abruptly—especially not by choice. Baseball had been my entire life. I had given up a lot for it.

I was the kid who missed prom because he was meeting with recruits. The kid who was one of the last in my class to get his driver's license because he was too busy training. The kid—and man—who let baseball be his whole identity. I also rarely went out on dates in high school—and after—because I traveled too much with the teams.

That kid was getting his second chance.

Everything was finally coming together—not just to make Cora mine, but to become a man she'd want to keep.

# 4

## Jay

*Twelve Years Ago*

At the start of my senior year, I was struggling. We were only three months into the school year and I was failing math and science. I wasn't dumb. I just had my priorities all wrong. My focus was on baseball, and only baseball.

Even though the fall wasn't high school baseball season, I still worked with my coach on conditioning. I had also been traveling with my dad most weekends to go look at colleges that had made me baseball scholarship offers.

My baseball coach was also my P.E. teacher, and he had pulled me aside after class one day, pissed. He informed me that I was failing two classes, and unless I got my grades up soon, I wouldn't be able to play baseball in the spring.

I'd never felt that level of dread in my entire life.

I knew I'd been falling behind, but I hadn't realized I was failing. He'd given me a note that had to be signed by my parents and returned the next day. I dreaded giving them that, and I'd thought about it the entire drive home. Even my sister had noticed my sour mood.

"What's got your panties in a twist today?" she asked from the passenger seat.

I told her about my meeting with Coach Jensen, and after her initial shock and giving me shit for it, she was actually very helpful.

"Why don't you just have Cora tutor you?" she said, as if this were the most obvious solution.

"What?"

"Cora...you know...my bestie! She's really freaking good at both those subjects. She literally has a one hundred in science right now," Morgan informed me. "And she has an A in math, too. Her foster moms won't let her get a job right now because they want her to focus on her schoolwork, so she would love to have the extra money you would pay her for tutoring you."

I thought about it and realized this could definitely work for both of us—I get my grades up, and she gets some spare cash. The only problem was that Cora was gorgeous.

Something had happened to her over the summer,

causing her to go from cute, girl-next-door nerd to sexy cover-model nerd.

Lately, whenever she came over to visit my sister, I found myself hanging out with them, playing board games, watching whatever stupid show they wanted to watch, or listening in on whatever gossip they had about boys in our school. I told myself it was because I was a guy and wanted to know what girls were saying about my friends and me. But if I were honest with myself, I knew my level of interest went beyond that.

Hearing them talk about other guys should have been no big deal. Teenage girls did that all the time. Hell, the girls in most of my classes talked nonstop about the guys in our grade. But hearing Cora do it had me seeing red. That realization should have scared me—I was only eighteen—but it didn't.

After my mom arranged everything—because she didn't trust me to do it myself—I met Cora after school in the library to start our first tutoring session. She was wearing jeans and an oversized teal sweatshirt that made her eyes seem brighter.

For the next thirty minutes, I struggled to focus on anything but her, which was why I was caught off guard when she asked me a question.

"Jay?"

"Sorry, what did you say?" I asked, shaking my head to clear my thoughts.

"What were you staring at?"

Before I could think better of it, I gave her the truth.

"Your hair looks really soft. I like it when you wear it down like that with your curls loose. It's really hot."

*Did I just say hot? Shit.*

I hadn't meant to say that. It was the truth, but that probably wasn't appropriate talk for your tutor and sister's best friend.

"Umm, thanks," she mumbled, her cheeks turning pink as she tucked her hair nervously behind her ear.

"Why don't we take a break," she suggested, which made me feel bad because I wasn't sure I had learned much, other than she had pretty handwriting and smelled wonderful.

"Okay, brain break means answering easy questions," she said, leaning back in her chair, clasping her hands in her lap. "Probably obvious, but what do you want to be after you graduate?"

She was right. That was definitely the easy to answer. "Professional baseball player, hands down."

She smiled at me and then tilted her head in thought. "Not trying to be a Debbie-Downer, but let's say that isn't an option for whatever reason. What's your backup plan?"

I knew what she meant without saying it. I could get injured, or maybe college baseball was the furthest my career would go.

"If I can't do the major leagues, then Dad wants me to go to college and get a degree in something useful, like business," I told her.

She stared at me for a few moments, and I wasn't sure

if she was going to say something or if I should ask her the same questions.

"Okay, but what do you want to do?" she asked finally. "Not what your dad *hopes* you will do, but what *you* want to do if professional baseball isn't in the cards for you."

I hadn't realized I'd said it that exact way until she mentioned it. I knew what my backup option was, but since my dad had kind of shot it down and told me to go to business school, I hadn't thought much more about it. But Cora felt like a safe space I could give that to.

"Firefighter. I'd like to be a firefighter and help people out." I may have said it simply, but my heart was racing, waiting for her to give me her thoughts, like I needed her approval.

"That's awesome!" Her face was filled with a huge, genuine smile, and it made me feel good seeing her excitement over it. "You'd be really good at that."

"Thanks." I felt a little uncomfortable at her praise since my own parents hadn't seemed nearly as excited.

"Oh, I know!" She clapped her hands and then reached down into her backpack for another book. "Let's review the section on wildfires and wind, cause that will be on the test."

"How do you know it will be on the test?" I asked since she wasn't in my class.

"It was on the study guide you gave me."

Ahh. That made sense.

"You didn't look at it?"

"Not yet," I said, putting my right hand on the back of my neck and rubbing it to cover my slight embarrassment.

We spent the next twenty minutes going over the study guide, and I really felt like it helped. She was really good at tutoring, or maybe I just found it easier to pay attention to her as opposed to my teacher.

"Have you ever heard of a fire rainbow?"

"No, but it sounds cool."

"Okay, well, despite the name, it's neither a rainbow, nor is it related to fire in any way."

I laughed. "Then why is it named that?"

"Probably for the same reason a jellyfish is neither a fish, nor is it made of jelly. People just like to come up with catchy names that sound cool."

I paused, taking in what she had just said, and laughed again. I hadn't realized she was so funny.

"The real name is circumhorizontal arc, and it's a type of sun halo, but from a distance it can sometimes look like fire with the nearby clouds looking like smoke."

"How do you know so much?" I asked her, finding myself wanting to learn more about her than about schoolwork.

"I'm fascinated by the weather," she said, flipping through the pages of her book in search of something. "My foster sister, Iris, and I love learning about it and teaching each other cool facts. The weather is always doing something crazy somewhere in the world at any given time."

She finally looked up at me, and I could see the thrill

in her eyes as she spoke. "There could be flooding in Japan, tornadoes in the U.S., a hurricane in Mexico, wildfires in Australia, or a blizzard in Europe."

"Is that what you want to be when you graduate? A weather person?"

"The term is meteorologist," she corrected me, but with a smile on her face, so I knew she was only teasing. "Iris definitely wants to be one, but I don't know. I love weather, but I also love geology, biology, and astronomy, so I'm not sure yet."

She was usually rather quiet, so it was interesting to see her so talkative and animated about something other than hair, makeup, and boys, like she talked about with my sister.

"I definitely want to be a scientist of some kind. I just don't know exactly what yet."

My inner thoughts immediately went to picturing her wearing a white lab coat and nothing else.

Every tutoring session we had over the next three months was filled with her teaching me, talking about our futures, favorite foods, teachers we liked and disliked, and me going home and picturing her naked underneath a lab coat.

"Oh my God, you got an A!" Cora's voice was filled with happiness and cheer as she looked at the graded test I'd just given her.

I felt a swell of pride at my accomplishment, but also because I had earned that beautiful smile of hers that was directed at me.

We were sitting on the floor in my room. She leaned in, gripping me in a tight hug. Not one to miss this opportunity, I wrapped my arms around her and pulled her close. Her chest was pressed up against me, and I had to focus to not get hard with her body pushing into mine.

"I knew you could do it." Her soft whisper was next to my ear. I wanted badly to just turn my head and kiss her cheek and then work my way down her neck and touch every inch of her body.

She pulled back, but I kept my gaze on hers. She released me from her arms, but while my grip had loosened, my hands remained at her hips, keeping her close.

She stared up at me with those big, beautiful eyes. I'd dreamed of watching those eyes flutter closed after I kissed her senseless.

I knew I needed a taste. I had to kiss her.

I moved slowly, giving her a chance to retreat, but she stayed still, her gaze boring into mine.

"Cora! Which dress looks better?" my sister's voice yelled from around the corner before she magically appeared in my doorway.

Cora's body had jolted the instant my sister said her name, and she pulled back from me.

I was going to murder my sister.

I growled. "We're studying, Morgan. Leave."

She waved me off like I was a fly in the room. "This is more important."

She turned to Cora, who now had her full attention. "Pink or blue?"

Cora watched as my sister swapped the two dresses back and forth in front of her.

"Pink," Cora responded.

"I knew it!"

"You have your choice. Now go away so we can finish," I ordered her.

Morgan rolled her eyes at me. "Ugh, whatever. Thanks, bestie!"

The instant she was gone, I turned back to Cora, hoping we could salvage the moment and go back to where I had left off.

"Now, where were we before Morgan rudely interrupted?" I grinned and watched as a small smile formed on her face and her cheeks turned pink.

"I was telling you how proud I was of you for your test score." Her smile brightened, and I loved seeing that directed at me.

"Is there a reward for that? I feel like there should be a reward for all my hard work."

She chuckled and then tilted her head in deep thought. "What did you have in mind?"

"I have a few ideas," I told her and started to lean closer to her again, just like I'd done a few moments ago.

"Jay! Cora!" my mom's voice hollered from downstairs. "Dinner's ready! Come on down before it gets cold."

That was it. Everyone in my family was going to be murdered tonight. All of them. Except the dog.

Cora hopped up from the floor. "We...uh...better go."

Thankfully, I had a few more tutoring sessions with Cora left, because there was no way I was just going to quit there.

I followed her downstairs to the kitchen. We sat down at the dinner table, Cora across from me, and I felt a swell of confidence and victory as she told my parents about my test score.

Despite everyone chiming in about my grades, the food, and our days in general, my focus rarely left the girl across from me. She was so close, yet not close enough.

It was torture, but I loved every minute of it.

# 5

## Cora

I didn't know what I did wrong in a past life, but it was clearly catching up to me now.

Specifically, this week, when I saw two guys from my past—two of whom I'd had a romantic interest with.

Six months ago, I had broken up with a guy—Darren—who I'd been seeing for about four months. He was the epitome of "don't judge a book by the cover"—cute on the outside, but a huge dickhead on the inside.

At first, he was nice and pleasant to be around. He was a scientist as well, and we had several other interests in common. But then he changed.

It started with simple comments about how I had to work weekends or holidays and I never had time for him. He worked as a professor at the local university, so he had weekends and all major holidays off, as well as all the random holidays only teachers, bankers, and politicians got to have. Well, I didn't have that luxury.

Mother Nature didn't take a chill pill simply because it was a Sunday or Thanksgiving, or even two in the morning on St. Patrick's Day an hour after you went to sleep after drinking your body weight in green beer.

It made me work weird hours, but I loved my job. Darren hadn't understood that, so I finally got smart and dumped his ass.

So, it was easy to understand why I hadn't been thrilled to walk up to the scene of a wildfire assessment earlier today and see my ex standing there.

Seriously, two guys in one week?

"Darren, what are you doing here?" I asked him.

"Cora, what a surprise!" Darren said, looking at me like this was anything *but* a surprise. "I work for BAER Teams now."

I paused, completely stunned by what he had just said. "You left your teaching job?"

"Yep," he replied as though it were that simple.

"You left your *stable* teaching job...with holidays and weekends off...to take a job working for the Burned Area Emergency Response Teams?" I repeated slowly, knowing I couldn't possibly have heard him correctly.

"That's what I just said," he said, looking at me like I was stupid. "My background as a soil scientist with experience in forestry management made me an ideal candidate. This will allow me to be a part of restoring these beautiful forests to the best they can be after fires."

*What the absolute fuck?*

So, I guessed when *I* worked weekends, it was a bad thing, but when *he* did it, then it was okay?

God, I was so happy I broke up with his stupid ass.

"Hi, I'm Jade," said my coworker, who had been watching the interaction, introducing herself to Darren. "I work with Cora."

While I mostly did these assessments on my own, today's had been one of what was suspected to be part of a string of arsons, so I'd brought someone else from our office along to assist. My job wasn't to determine who'd started the fire, but to evaluate how severe the burn impacts were onto the soil when it came to landscape stability. Things like that were used to predict floods, debris flows, and water contamination.

"I'm Darren Derikson," he responded, smiling at Jade. "I work with BAER, and I'm happy to help you with *anything* you might need."

God, what a douche-canoe. It took everything in me not to roll my eyes at his comment.

"That's so sweet of you," she replied with a smile. "Thank you so much."

Jade reminded me a lot of my sister, Hazel. She was small but mighty. Jade was just a few inches over five feet and had a bold personality. Where she differed from my sister was that she had platinum blonde hair full of curls —a riot of them that matched her character.

Jade and I not only worked together. We had also hung out a few times with other coworkers. However, while she knew a bit about my dating history, she probably didn't realize this was the same Darren I'd dated last year.

We spent the following two hours working together to prepare an assessment for the area on debris flow and erosion potential after the wildfire that burned through this area several days ago.

I snapped pictures and took measurements, all while watching him stare at my ass the whole time.

What a creep.

Even before Darren, my dating history hadn't exactly produced any winners. Needless to say, I hadn't wanted to get back into the dating pool again so quickly, but my sister by blood, Hazel, as well as my sister-from-another-mister, Iris, had both told me to just put myself out there and see. Mr. Right could be just around the corner.

So, I did. Sort of.

When Jay sent me a message last night asking if I wanted to get breakfast with him on Monday, I decided to go for it. However, I would be driving myself. I wanted that choice in case I embarrassed myself beyond repair. It wasn't every day that you got to have a breakfast date with the guy you had dreamed about for more than a decade.

The problem was, I'd done nothing but freak out ever since about said date, so I decided to go home and try to get some work done. Jade was great, but after we'd gone back to the office, all she kept talking about was Darren and Bernard with BAER, which made me think of my crappy dating life and whether or not Jay would just be another name on that list of guys I'd gone on a date with that didn't work out.

I figured going home would let me see if working from a different environment would be better. My apartment was nothing to write home about. I lived in Sunny Valley, which was a small suburb outside Reno. It was far enough out of the city that I had quiet but still lived close to work.

My apartment was part of a two-story stucco complex, and I lived on the top floor in a spacious one-bedroom unit. It was an open floor plan, nine-hundred square foot space and had a cute little covered balcony that was great to sit outside on when it wasn't a million degrees like today.

My office was really just my dining room, but it had a big window, so it made it feel nice and bright, even though the space itself wasn't a true office.

I sat at my big oak table, scrolling through data on some soil samples from recent burn scars, assessing their flooding potential. Usually, I could get lost in information like that. I loved science, especially environmental science, and I loved studying the quiet ways that water shaped our world.

Most people wouldn't think of fires and floods as connected, but they were often interdependent.

Jay fought the flames, and I studied what survived them.

And there I was, thinking about Jay again.

I sighed. This was useless.

After hours of failed attempts to distract myself with work, I decided it was time to call in reinforcements—I needed advice.

Iris answered immediately after it rang once. "Hey girl, what's up?"

"You helped get me into this mess, so you're going to help me get through it." I skipped my usual greeting, choosing instead to just jump right into things.

She chuckled before asking for clarification. "Okay, well, I get you into a lot of messes, so you're going to have to be more specific."

"My date with Jay! He texted and asked me out to breakfast on Monday and then to go shopping for his groomsman's tux for his sister's wedding. What do I do?" I practically pleaded for advice.

"Wear sexy panties!" I heard an elderly voice yell into the phone, followed by Iris's laugh.

"You're on speakerphone, by the way, and Nancy says wear sexy panties."

Great. Nancy was Iris's next-door neighbor and one of my favorite people. She was pushing eighty years old but acted fifty years younger.

Nancy was a bestselling romance author and always gave us advice on men—though most of it was about sex. She had given us copies of several of her books—ones she felt fit us individually—and highlighted certain parts that she wanted us to know about.

"Hi, Nancy," I greeted her.

"So, are you just picking up his clothes, or going together to watch him try them on?" Iris asked, breaking me out of my thoughts.

"Oooo, changing room sex," Nancy's voice cooed. "I've never tried that, but that could be a fun one. If you do it, let me know how it goes. I may add that into my next book."

I ignored her comment because I was not going to have sex with Jay on our first date, nor was I going to have sex in a changing room.

"I think he's like most guys and probably waited until the last minute to order it," I explained in lieu of answering Nancy's request.

"Isn't her wedding next month?" Iris's shocked voice broke in.

"Yes, it is, but I need you to focus, sis. What do I do here?"

"You can tell a lot by how he acts when he picks you up," Nancy confided. "Does he come up to your door or just honk from his car and make you walk out to him? Does he bring you flowers, or at least have a big smile on his face when you open the door?"

"I'm actually meeting him at the restaurant, and then we'll walk across the street to the bridal store when we're done," I explained.

"He didn't offer to pick you up?" Iris asked, seemingly shocked.

"He did, but I prefer to drive so I'm not reliant on him if I need to bail." I tried to defend my reasoning, but even listening to myself, it sounded like a weak excuse.

"You modern women and your insistence on driving yourselves everywhere," Nancy grumbled. "You've heard the expression *'why buy the cow when you're giving the milk away for free'*? This is before all that. If you want a good man, you've gotta see how he treats the cow. Does he transport it everywhere it needs to go? Take care of it when it's sick?" She paused and then added in a sultry voice, "And—most importantly—does he know how to massage the beef in all the right places?"

I wasn't sure about that last one, and clearly neither was Iris, since I heard her giggle.

"I think what Nancy is *trying* to say is, if he offered to pick you up, let him. Give him the chance to show you whether he can be a good man or not. If you take away those opportunities from him, it will make it harder for you to see if he's a good man."

I chatted with them for the next few minutes as they gave me their guidance and suggestions. Despite Nancy's advice—which mostly pertained to what to wear and how to get him naked by the end of the night—and Iris's pointers on how to not embarrass myself, I was still nervous as hell.

I debated texting the rest of my sisters, but hesitated and chose to only text Hazel instead. I didn't need all of them ganging up on me with their directives.

ME:

Hey sis, guess what?

HAZEL:

Chicken butt :P

I rolled my eyes at her stupid retort, but that was Hazel. She was goofy but also had the most outgoing, bubbly personality of everyone in our family. In total, there were more than fifteen girls the O'Hara women had fostered, but only five of us had stayed permanently—Gale, Iris, Anna, Hazel, and me.

A few pings on my phone startled me out of my thoughts.

HAZEL:

You ever gonna tell me?

HAZEL:

Or do I get to keep on guessing?

ME:

Do you remember Morgan's brother Jay?

HAZEL:

The one you had the hots for and kissed
right before he left?

Okay, so apparently telling your sister everything had its pitfalls.

ME:

He lives in Reno now, apparently, and he
asked me out to breakfast...on a date

HAZEL:

I know. Iris already told me. ☺

*What the hell?*

Iris had the biggest mouth.

HAZEL:

I didn't say anything to you because I
wasn't sure if you were going to say yes
since you usually chicken out on these
things.

Sometimes it wasn't a good thing to have your sister know you so well.

HAZEL:

Plus, we got a new octopus a few days
ago, and he is becoming the biggest
pain in my ass.

Hazel worked at an aquarium and marine rescue center and was always bringing in new animals. Normally, I would love to talk with her about it, but right now my nerves were at an all-time high.

ME:

Well, I said yes.

HAZEL:

And now you're panicking.

Yep, she definitely knew me too well.

My phone vibrated in my hand as it showed Hazel was calling.

"Hey," I answered, trying to sound like my usual self, but I was happy she couldn't see my face right now, or she would notice the anxiety written all over it.

She sighed and exhaled a big breath. "Okay, yes, you're panicking, but this isn't a bad thing."

Well, there went my attempt to hide my anxiousness.

"Hey. Breathe." Her voice was soothing and patient. "It's just breakfast, not a marriage proposal. You said yes—and that's already a huge step for you. I'm proud of you, Cora."

"Thanks, Hazel."

"So, talk to me. What are you nervous about?"

"I'm worried I'll freeze up. Or say something stupid. Or that he'll realize I'm not the girl he remembers and wonder why he even asked me out."

She took a deep breath as though she was about to lay it all out for me. "Okay, there's a lot to unpack there, but let's start with the first thing. If you freeze up, bring up Morgan."

"Morgan? Why?" I asked.

"Because you know her really well, and so does he, but it's a neutral topic that you both can discuss."

Okay, that made a lot of sense, and yes, Morgan was certainly a safe topic.

"Second, you *aren't* the same girl from high school. Neither am I," she explained. "None of us are, Cora, but that's okay. People change, but that doesn't mean it's a bad thing. You've changed, and so has Morgan, but you are both still friends. Change isn't bad, so stop worrying about it. Maybe he'll love the changes and will love you even more now than he did back in school, and you'll get married and live in a cute house and have eight babies and live happily ever after."

"*Eight* kids?" My voice squeaked as I repeated her comment.

She chuckled, letting me know she was just messing with me.

I exhaled, starting to feel calmer, but I still had one more intrusive thought to get through.

"What if I've built him up too much in my head over the years?" I asked her but didn't give her time to respond before continuing my thought. "I've been crushing on this man for years, Hazel. What if the reality doesn't match the version I've been carrying around since high school?"

"You've got this," she replied, ever the positive one. "Look, if I can handle an octopus with attitude and anger-management issues, you can handle one breakfast date with your dream man."

I chuckled at her amazing ability to not only calm me but also make me laugh when I was having my panic episodes.

"I believe in you, sis," she told me just before a loud noise crashed in the background. "Goddammit, Nigel. I've got to go murder an octopus. Call me after your date, and you can tell me all the details."

"I will. Love you," I told her as a shrill beeping noise carried through the phone.

"Shit. Love you too. Bye." Her last word was cut off as

the call ended, and I felt slightly bad about not asking for more details about this new devious octopus.

I made a mental note to ask her about it when I called her on Monday after my date.

A date that I now was feeling very excited—and hardly nervous at all—about.

Mostly.

Monday came fast, and as I sat in a booth at the restaurant, my nerves kicked up every minute that went by.

It was ten minutes past eight, and Jay still wasn't here. I knew it was only ten minutes, but something felt off. I mean, shouldn't he have texted if he was going to be late? I would have.

It wasn't easy to park around here, so maybe he was just circling around trying to find a spot. At least, that was what I told myself.

"Can I get you something to drink while you wait?" the friendly waitress asked me.

I'd gotten here a few minutes ago and decided to get a table in case the place got busy, because this was a popular restaurant.

"Um, sure. I'll take a coffee, please," I told her.

I pulled out my phone, double checking that this was the only Friends With Benedicts restaurant location and I hadn't gone to the wrong one by mistake. I knew it wasn't likely, since the bridal shop was across the street, but I just needed to check for my own sanity.

After pulling it up on my phone to confirm that this was, in fact, the only location, I started to get worried. What if he was in an accident? What if he'd worked last night and gotten stuck at a fire?

I had no idea what his hours were or how his schedule worked. I knew I could text Morgan, but I wasn't ready for her to know we were on a date. Morgan had tried to see if I was interested in her brother for years so we could one day be real sisters, but once her brother left the state to play baseball—and took my heart with him—I tried to play it cool and pretend I had no interest. I did that for myself just as much as I had for Morgan.

I knew if I texted her and told her we were going on a date, even if it was just breakfast, she would get excited, and it would get my hopes up. Hopes that I didn't want to come crashing down if he left like the last time. No, it was better to just wait it out before I said anything to her. I was going to have to tread lightly with this one. But even as I thought about it, I realized that would be a difficult prospect since I was already half in love with this man and had been since high school.

The waitress brought my coffee and set it down with some sugar and creamer. "Are you ready to order yet, or do you want to wait for your other person to arrive?" she asked, pointing at the menu across from me.

I didn't know how to answer because he should be here by now, but I didn't want to chance it in case he'd gotten stuck in traffic or something and I came off as rude if I ordered without him. "I'll just wait a few more minutes. Thank you."

She nodded and walked away, and I checked my phone again—for the thirtieth time in the last ten minutes.

I finally decided to text him, just to check.

ME:

Just checking in...

Another ten minutes went by, and there was still no response. I didn't know whether to be worried or pissed, but worrying that this could be from something going wrong, I decided to go with checking on his wellbeing.

ME:

Are you okay?

Now it was eight thirty, and I realized I couldn't keep holding up a table, so I finally placed my order.

I did it so that I could make it worth my waitress's time so she wasn't just getting a dollar tip from me for one single coffee. I also did it because I was now reeling with emotions at the likelihood of being stood up, and I needed food to give me energy.

Twenty minutes later, my meal was finished, and there was still no response from Jay. Unless something terrible had happened, it was looking more and more like I had been stood up.

It took everything I had not to cry once I made it out

to my car. The man I had dreamed about since high school had finally asked me out on a date, and then he'd stood me up.

My phone chimed with a new text, and I whipped it out so fast I almost hit myself in the face.

My heart raced as I tapped on the screen to see Jay's name—only it wasn't. It was Iris's name instead.

IRIS:

Call me as soon as your "date" is done so you can tell me all about it. I'm working from home today and Hector is at the office, so you can call me anytime! But also, take your time with him. Enjoy it!

My heart pinched. I was both sad that it wasn't Jay texting me and also wounded with pride that I was going to have to tell my sister what happened, but I wasn't ready to talk to her about it yet. I decided that instead of just going home right away, I would distract myself by running some errands, maybe treat myself to a new book at the bookstore, and then go home and eat a pint of ice cream for dinner.

I sent her a text to give her a quick update.

ME:

It didn't go exactly as planned. I'm okay, but I've got a few things I need to do. I'll call you later, I promise.

# 6

**"I know there's something wrong with my cactus.
I just can't quite put my finger on it."**
—*It's science*

## Cora

*Twelve Years Ago*

My family and my best friend Morgan were the only ones who knew that I had been held back in school. When we were younger, our father had neglected to make sure Hazel and I always went to school. This resulted in home-work not being turned in, reports not being completed, and tests not being taken.

When Hazel and I moved in with the O'Haras, our case worker had us tested before we went to our new school. While I'd passed, barely, Mom and Auntie were worried. Starting high school in a new place was already an intense situation. Plus, we had the trauma of being uprooted and placed with a new family on the other side of the state. They didn't want me struggling with school-work, adding another layer of stress. They sat me down and walked me through the pros and cons together until we figured out what made the most sense.

Thankfully, my birthday was in the summer, so most kids just thought I was really old for my grade and didn't realize I had been held back.

This meant Jay and I were actually only about six months apart in age.

Morgan swore to me that she never told anyone my secret, but there were times it was a bit awkward—at least for me—when I would be tutoring Jay and realized I could potentially have been in his classes, had I stayed in my original grade.

I often thought about what it would be like to sit next to him in class—better yet, behind him, so that I could stare at him without him knowing.

"Cora."

Startled, I shook my head. "What?"

Jay just smiled at me, like he knew exactly what I was thinking. "I asked if you're more of a cat person or a dog person."

"Oh."

At least this was an easy question.

"Both. I like all animals, really, but if I had to pick one, I would say cats. They're easier to handle if you can't be home all the time. I would feel less guilty if I had to work late or something."

"That makes sense." He smiled at me as he often did whenever he learned something about me. We usually didn't talk about particularly deep topics, but he always seemed so interested in every answer I gave.

"What about you?" I asked in return.

"Definitely a dog, but I would also feel guilty about never being home enough to give it the attention it needed. I'm probably more suited for, like, a fish or something, or whatever animal you don't really have to pay a lot of attention to."

"All animals need attention," I told him. Working on the O'Haras' farm had taught me that. Even animals you didn't think required a lot of work often still wanted attention, or they would get into trouble.

"I know. I just want something that I can go a few days without feeding it or walking it and still have it be fine."

"I believe you are referring to a plant," I deadpanned, and he chuckled. "Maybe a cactus would be better for you to start with."

"Alright, funny girl, I get your point."

It was the summer after our junior year, and Morgan and I had filled our night with a pop music marathon, face masks we were convinced would keep us looking young forever, and a pile of junk food. We had tried to do each other's makeup, but we'd ended up looking like clowns who'd lost a fight with a glitter bomb. Finally, Morgan declared she was too "emotionally exhausted," and we passed out on her bed.

Sometime after one a.m., I woke up to a dry mouth and a full bladder. I shuffled to the bathroom quickly and then made my way downstairs to the Rainers' kitchen, hoping to get a glass of water.

The house was silent except for the hum of the fridge, but as I turned the corner, there he was—Jay.

He was leaning against the counter, shirtless, wearing only gray sweatpants, and his hair looked damp, like he had just taken a shower. He was holding a glass of water and looked up when I walked in. His eyes were sleepy and way too attractive for this hour.

"Hey," he said, his voice rough. "I didn't wake you, did I?"

"No. I couldn't sleep," I lied as I stared at his sexy frame before me.

I wasn't about to tell him I had to pee—how embarrassing.

I was so into Jay, it was scary. I may or may not have written my name as Mrs. Cora Rainer in my diary a few times. A few dozen times. But he didn't need to know that.

"I uh, just needed a cup of you...I mean...a cup of water."

I had talked with Jay a lot over the last year, but apparently now my brain was incapable of coherent thoughts around him.

He smiled and nodded, but he kept staring at me for a moment before finally pushing off the counter to grab a glass for me. Instead of handing it to me right away, he filled it and then turned back to me. His fingers brushed over mine as he handed me the glass, igniting a tiny spark that lit up my whole arm.

We both stood there for a second, just looking at each other. No words, just the quiet hum of the house and the knowledge that we were both awake when everyone else was asleep. Alone and very aware of how close we were.

"You're not still in a tizzy about Morgan and me borrowing your sound system for our impromptu karaoke session, are you?" I asked, since he was staring so hard at me, now without a smile.

He shook his head. "No, but I am in a tizzy about something else."

He took one small step closer to me, and I licked my lips, thinking of what it would feel like to have him kiss me.

"Wha…" I cleared the frog in my throat. "What, um, are you in a tizzy about?"

"Trying to decide if I should kiss you," he said quietly, his dark gaze never leaving mine.

My breath caught in my chest, and I did a double take.

*Did I hear him correctly? Did he just say he wanted to kiss me?*

I wanted to pinch my arm to see if this was real or a dream, but that would be super awkward if this was real.

*Play it cool.*

"Ummm…sure, I guess."

*Oh my God. I was an idiot.*

*I guess? Who says that?*

He smirked and then leaned over and kissed me. It was gentle at first, even sweet, but that quickly turned into a savage meeting between our mouths.

My back was up against the counter as my hands moved of their own free will to his chest. He moved his hands to my hips and then under my shirt. His hands were warm. I don't know who ended up doing it first, but we pulled each other impossibly closer as my fingers tangled in his hair.

His mouth was hot and hungry against mine. We were both breathing fast, hearts pounding, the world outside the kitchen completely forgotten. He tasted like mint and root beer. It was a weird combination, but it tasted delicious.

Just then, a whisper yell from the stairs broke our intense moment.

"Cora, are you down there?" Morgan's voice was muffled but still floated down the stairs.

We both froze.

Jay pulled back, eyes wide, breathless but still holding me close.

"Sweet dreams, Cora," he whispered as he kissed my forehead, soft and quick like a promise, and then he turned quickly and walked down the hallway, bare feet silent on the wood.

I watched him go as my heart raced and my lips tingled.

It didn't matter that he was the type of guy who should have a warning label for being a danger to my heart. A girl still wanted to be wanted. It felt good when a hot man wanted to be with you. Especially one you'd dreamed about nearly every night.

# 7

## Jay

I was getting ready for my date with Cora when my phone buzzed. Morgan's name popped up, and I was happy to take the call, even though I was running a few minutes behind, because I needed to know what I was picking up, suit-wise, today.

"Hey, favorite sister," I greeted her.

She grumbled, but I could still hear the smile in her voice. "I'm your only sister."

"Semantics," I replied. "Hey, I'm about to head out the door, and I'm going to hit up the suit shop today to get what I need for your wedding. Can you text me the names of the styles and colors you picked again so I can make sure I get the right thing?"

"Yes, that's why I was calling. I was going to have you write it down on a piece of paper and repeat it back to me so I knew you got it, but that works too. I'll text it to you right now."

"Thanks, appreciate it," I told her and was just about to hang up when she shouted quickly into the phone.

"Send pictures of the receipt, or I won't believe you went!"

I rolled my eyes but smiled. Maybe I could have Cora take a few pictures of me—an excuse to keep her close and maybe bring her into the changing room with me.

My smile morphed into a wicked grin just thinking about it.

My phone buzzed again almost as soon as I put it down. I really didn't have time to answer it, or I was going to be late to meet Cora, but the minute I saw *Sawyer Stetson*—my boss's name—on the screen, I knew I couldn't ignore the call. It wasn't a good sign for him to be calling, because I knew that meant I was about to get roped into something. However, I was trying to work my way up through the ranks, so I picked up.

"Hey, Jay," he said after I greeted him. "I hate to do this to you on your day off, but the puke flu has been going around, and I'm down three firefighters today for the shift."

Shit. I did not want to miss my date with Cora.

"I've got someone coming in for the back half of the twenty-four-hour shift, but I need someone for the first twelve," he added, which meant I would definitely be missing the date since I needed to pivot to work.

"It sucks, I get that, but you coming in for stuff like

this doesn't go unnoticed by Leavenworth," he said, mentioning the assistant fire chief's name. "This is the kind of teamwork he remembers when looking at your application for investigator."

I hated it, but I knew he was right. I was so close to getting this job I could taste it. I would make it up to Cora somehow, because I couldn't pass this up, not when there was so much on the line.

"Yeah, no problem," I told him. "Let me grab my bag, and I'll be in."

"Thanks, Jay," he replied, sounding relieved. "I'm meeting with Leavenworth later today and will definitely mention this."

After I hung up with him, I shot off a quick text to Cora to let her know I got called into work and wouldn't be able to meet for breakfast, but I would make it up to her.

I kept hoping it would be a slow shift so I could text back and forth with Cora and maybe even talk on the phone a little to make up for bailing on our date, but today had turned into an absolutely insane shift.

Cora had texted me shortly after I had gotten on shift, something about "just checking on me" or something like that, which I thought was sweet, but I hadn't had time to respond since it was a shit show from the moment I walked into the station.

First, there was an accident on the highway that required our EMS crew, the fire engine, and the jaws of life. Thankfully, everyone was okay, but that had happened about ten minutes after I walked into the firehouse.

Next up, it was a false alarm at a school because some kids didn't feel like taking their math test. That wasn't a particularly hard call, but we got the call as we were still driving back from the accident.

After that, it was an actual fire at an abandoned warehouse. Teenagers were smoking and had thrown their leftover butts in the dry shrubs next to the building, not realizing they would spark and set the whole place on fire.

That callout had required three separate engines to assist since it was hot and dry outside, and the fire had spread quickly. It also took over three hours to put out and finalize the scene. By the time we got back to the station, I was wiped the fuck out and chose to catch a quick nap with a few of the other guys.

Later, once I finally came off shift, I pulled out my phone to see I had missed texts from my sister and Cora, as well as my cousin, Mack. Knowing Mack only ever communicated in memes, and my sister was likely texting to check in on me about the suit that I never got a chance to go get, I went to the text from Cora first. Also, I just found myself wanting to read hers first anyway because I knew it would make me smile.

CORA:

Are you okay?

That was sweet of her to worry. I wanted to think of something funny to write back, so I decided to go see what my sister wrote first while I thought of something to text Cora back with.

MORGAN:

Umm…are you in town? Cause I didn't
realize we were having breakfast today.
Or do you mean a different day?

*What?*

*Oh shit.*

My heart started racing as I connected the dots.

I looked at the previous message and realized I had texted Morgan about missing breakfast instead of Cora.

I quickly jumped back over to that text thread, and sure enough, I hadn't sent Cora anything. Not a single thing.

Shit.

The "are you okay" was probably because she thought something bad happened because I stood her up. And her previous text of "just checking in" was likely to find out why I was late.

Double shit.

This was not going like I had planned.

I immediately called her as I got into my truck. This apology could not be done via text. Hell, if I'd known where she lived, I would have driven over to her place to apologize.

My heart raced as the phone began to ring. Each subsequent ring had my heart picking up the pace just a little more.

She didn't answer, so I was forced to leave a voicemail. I felt deflated and defeated but knew this was my only chance to try to make this right.

"Hey, Cora. It's Jay. I'm so sorry about today. I messed up. Bad. I got called into work to cover for a sick coworker, and I sent you a text explaining all of that, but I accidentally sent it to my sister. Morgan replied all confused, and then that's when I realized I texted her instead of you. I feel terrible. Worse than I did when I realized I had to get a raincheck for our date. I'm back on a twenty-four-hour shift tomorrow but then off again for forty-eight. I would love to take you out and make up for this. I'm so sorry. I'll make it right, I swear. Just...please call me back."

I hung up. My thumb hovered over the screen like I could somehow magically will her name to appear.

Cora was a sweet person, so I was banking on the fact that maybe she would understand once she heard my explanation.

After years of wanting this moment to happen— finally taking her out on a date—I had screwed it up. I just had to hope that I hadn't screwed up so badly that she wasn't willing to give me another chance.

Just then, a new idea came to me.

I grabbed my phone and placed the call.

"Hey, bro. What was with the weird message earlier?" Morgan asked. "I thought you were meeting my bestie?"

"I don't have a lot of time to explain, but I need you to give me Cora's address. Please." I added the polite word at the end because this was an emergency and I needed to pull out all the stops.

Desperate times called for desperate measures.

# 8

**"Will I regret this? Probably.**

**Will I still do it anyway? 100%."**

—*It's science*

## Jay

*Twelve Years Ago*

I kissed Cora.

After all those times seeing her on the couch in my house, or across from me at the table in the school library, tempting me with her cute body, her sharp wit, and infectious laugh, I finally kissed her.

It wasn't a simple kiss either. I kissed her like I was starved and was getting my first meal after days without one. It was everything I had always thought it would be with her—fiery, electric, and incredible.

The touch of her soft skin under my fingers as I slid them up her shirt felt like a dream.

She shivered at my touch, and it wasn't because she was cold. Her skin was soft but on fire. If she shivered at my mere touch, what would she do when I put my mouth all over her?

I felt my dick getting harder by the second, aching to be closer to her and rub up against her.

Then my sister ruined it all by coming to get her from the kitchen.

I told her goodnight and then had to quickly walk away, or I was going to embarrass myself.

I walked down the hall to the small bathroom just to get my shit together. I splashed cold water on my face, but what I really needed was a cold shower.

That kiss had been incredible. My fingers tingled at the memory of what her skin had felt like. I had just made it to where my fingers brushed over her bra when Morgan had called out.

I groaned at her impeccable timing for cockblocking.

I spent the next twenty-four hours thinking about how my life was going to change. I was told by Coach Jensen and an adviser that I had a good chance of being picked in the fourth, fifth, or sixth round of the draft. More importantly, the San Francisco team wanted me, which was super close to home. I could play for their minor league team and still be close enough to try things out with Cora.

After that kiss, I knew I wanted to ask her out. I'd debated it for months but had hesitated because I wasn't sure what was going to happen after graduation.

I told myself to wait two more days until the draft, and

once everything was signed and set, I would tell her the good news and ask her out.

Granted, if things didn't work out and I didn't get drafted, my backup plan was to take the baseball scholarship from UCLA. That would be farther away, but still doable.

Two days later, my life changed forever.

Everything happened quickly.

My dad and I were sitting in the living room watching the draft take place live on TV. Morgan and my mom were in the kitchen cooking, but close enough in case I got a phone call.

I was nervous, so I got up to get a snack.

"Hey! I'm not finished with that." Morgan slapped my hand away from the platter she was making.

"Hey, is Cora coming over today?" I tried to ask casually. She had been over here nearly every day this summer, so it wasn't out of the ordinary for me to assume that.

"No, her family drove down to L.A. to go to Disneyland for a few days. Which sucks because it would have been so nice to have her here with me during your boring draft thing."

I rolled my eyes at her teasing, but I agreed with her on the fact that it would have been nice to have her here with us. Mostly because I wanted her here to celebrate with me.

As I walked back into the living room, my phone buzzed in my pocket. It showed an unknown number, but

I had a good feeling about it, so I answered and immediately put it on speaker so my dad could hear too.

"Hello," I answered.

"Jay Rainer?" the voice on the other end asked.

"Yes, this is Jay."

"My name is James Floyd, and I'm the general manager here for the team in Houston. Just wanted to let you know that we're drafting you with our next pick in the second round."

I said nothing as my eyes practically bulged out of my face. My gaze went directly to my dad.

"You there?" he said at my silence.

"Uh, yes. Sorry, sir. I didn't think your team had a need for another pitcher, so I'm just a little shocked, that's all," I explained to him, trying to play off my shock.

"In the last week, we've lost two pitchers to call-ups to the majors and two more to injuries, so we need another pitcher in a bad way."

I'd heard they'd had some players drop off their roster but hadn't realized it was that bad.

"It also means we would need you to come out here sooner rather than later," he added.

My mind was swirling as he gave more details over the phone. My dad took over talking as he handled most of the negotiations.

Within forty-eight hours, I went from thinking I was going to play baseball in California nearby to being drafted and signing with a team in Houston and hopping on a plane to begin practicing.

It was exciting as hell, and I loved every minute of it, except for one thing—Cora.

Because she was in Disneyland, I hadn't been able to see her before I left.

I knew I wanted more with Cora—more kissing, more movies, and more late-night chats, maybe even some naked chats. But she also needed to finish school.

I struggled all night with what to do. Did we try the long-distance thing while I was away? Did I try to get her to apply to schools in Texas and attend college there instead of in California?

Was I getting ahead of myself? Probably. Hell, Cora had just turned eighteen, and I wasn't far from nineteen myself. Obsessing over a woman I'd had one kiss with—even if it was amazing—seemed a bit extreme.

Over the next two weeks of practice, my mind was focused on the team and moving into a new place. But most nights, alone in my new apartment, I spent thinking of her. There were so many times I'd see someone up in the stands who looked like her and wished it was.

"You keep staring up at the stands, you're gonna get a foul ball to the face, Rainer," my teammate Vargas muttered beside me, his eyebrow lifted in question.

I blinked. "What?"

My neck had been craned to look out into the audience while our team was at bat.

"You keep looking up there like you're waiting for someone to show up." Vargas grinned at me as we stood up against the front railing of the dugout.

"Nah, just looking," I lied.

I *was* waiting, but I was waiting for something that would never happen.

"Ahhh, so you're scoping out the ladies," he teased, a small grin on his face. "Talk to Herrera first. He'll point out the crazy ones that you don't want to mess around with. Unless, of course, you like the stalker type."

"Uh, no. I'll check with him, thanks."

I wouldn't, but he didn't need to know that. I turned my gaze back to the game to try to refocus.

Four months later, I sat in my cab headed to the stadium, my cell phone in hand. I typed out and deleted at least six different messages to my sister. Messages I wanted her to pass along to Cora. But I just couldn't quite seem to get the words right.

I tried dating other women, telling myself it was just infatuation. That if I found someone new, I'd get over her, but no one ever held my attention like she had.

Hell, even when she was tutoring me, talking about schoolwork—literally the last thing I ever wanted to think about—she managed to keep my attention at all times.

No one challenged me like she did. Most women saw the uniform first, the sexy, glamorous life of it. Cora was the only one who had ever seen me—and that was the part no other woman could seem to fill.

There were hundreds of times my fingers itched to ask Morgan for Cora's phone number, but I never did.

What would I even say? The longer it went on, the

more I struggled internally with how to message her out of the blue when I hadn't given her an explanation.

We were headed to the AAA World Series, and I had wanted my sister to bring Cora with her. I wanted to see her in the stands cheering me on. I wanted her there to celebrate with me.

The stadium lights flared to life as the cab pulled up, and I realized the cruel irony of it all.

I was finally living my dream, and the one person I wanted to share it with most wasn't there.

Turned out that chasing your dream didn't mean you stopped missing the people you left behind. Success never felt so lonely.

# 9

—*It's science*

## Cora

It was time. I had waited long enough. I knew the longer I waited, the more antsy Iris would get, and she would eventually just hop on a plane or get in her car and drive up here.

I picked up my phone and texted her back.

ME:

> I should have listened to you and Nancy and let him drive me. That way, when he didn't show up, I could just sit alone at my place rather than alone at the restaurant like a fool for 30 minutes.

Five minutes later, my phone buzzed and Iris's name showed up on the screen as a FaceTime request.

Since I was just sitting on my couch, I decided to take

the call. What I hadn't expected was both Iris's and Nancy's faces to pop up on screen.

"What happened?" Iris asked, shock and a little bit of anger on her face.

"Tell us everything," Nancy all but demanded.

I explained what had happened this morning, trying to look at Nancy's face or down at my lap instead of looking at Iris. She was terrible at hiding her emotions. She had one of those faces that couldn't hide a thing. You knew exactly what she was thinking without ever saying a word.

"I'm sorry, Cora. I...well..." Iris said, causing me to glance up and see the look on her face.

"Iris, you're doing it again." I sighed, wondering if it had been a bad idea to accept the video call.

"It's true, dear," Nancy added, looking at her. "Your mouth can keep quiet, but your face cannot."

"Do you want me to come up there?" Iris asked. "I can work remotely, and that way you don't have to be alone."

"I appreciate it, but it's too far to drive. Plus, what about Hector? I'm pretty sure you should be spending time with him right now."

"Hector is still at work, but even if he wasn't, sister problems take precedent," Iris argued, making me give a small smile at the fact that I was blessed to have been given such awesome bonus sisters in my life.

"Exactly. Iris, get your car. I've got matches and rope. We ride at dawn!" Nancy's exuberant call to action caused Iris to throw her head back and laugh, but I just gave a weak smile since I wasn't entirely sure Nancy was joking.

I watched as Nancy's face left the frame and Iris's gaze turned to follow her, and then she just shook her head and grinned as if she didn't know what to do.

"Why don't you go take a hot shower, grab a good book to read, and just relax for the rest of the night," Iris suggested, and it sounded like a great idea.

"Yeah, you're probably right."

"I usually am," she teased, pausing as a new thought came to her. "Did you try reaching out to Morgan to make sure something serious didn't happen?"

"No, but I should," I told her.

"Give him twenty-four hours," she said. "Just in case. If you don't hear anything after that, then I'll personally help you get rid of him."

She gave me her best wicked smile, and I chuckled.

"I can't kill my best friend's brother, Iris," I quipped, noticing her facial expression change to concerned, perhaps borderline scared, as a loud noise sounded close to her.

"Well...judging by what Nancy is dragging out of her apartment right now, I think she might be planning to take care of this for you all on her own."

My eyes grew large and my mouth opened at her comment.

"Umm...I need to let you go," Iris said, her face still pointed in the direction of where I guessed Nancy was. "If she calls you...don't answer. Love you. I'll call you tomorrow."

I was about to tell her I loved her back, only to hear her yell at Nancy to stop, and then the phone call ended.

I sat there, stunned and slightly nervous about what Nancy was doing. I decided a hot shower was calling my name, so I got up and made my way to my room.

My phone rang no more than sixty seconds after I set it down on my nightstand to charge. Knowing it was likely Nancy, I decided to just let it go to voicemail and made my way to my bathroom instead.

Twenty minutes later, I had my wet hair wrapped up in a towel on top of my head and my thick, soft robe wrapped around my body, and I grabbed my phone to head into the kitchen to make myself a cup of tea.

Tapping the screen, I noticed a missed call and text. I stopped dead in my tracks as I stared at the name on the screen.

Jay.

I opened his voicemail and listened to his message several times.

He hadn't meant to ghost me.

I wanted to be mad at him for what had happened, but I also understood. My own job did that sometimes, and so did Iris's. It was the nature of the beast when you worked in careers that required people twenty-four-seven.

I broke up with the last guy I dated because he hadn't understood this. It would be entirely unfair for me to be pissed at Jay for that same reason.

My phone buzzed in my hand, but it was Morgan's name, not Jay's. I answered the call quickly.

"Hey," I greeted her.

"Cora," she said quickly into the phone, sounding very rushed and urgent. "I don't know how much time I have, so you have to talk fast, but my brother is on his way to your house."

Her tone implied she wasn't supposed to tell me that.

"What?" I asked, hoping I had heard her wrong.

"Where are you? Are you at your house?" she began asking questions in rapid-fire, leaving me no ability to respond. "He's on his way there! He said you were supposed to have breakfast together—for a date! Which... how could you not tell me!"

That last part ended on a screech, causing me to pull the phone away from my ear.

"Why is he coming here?" I asked her. "How does he know where I live?"

"I told him because he said he needed to apologize in person for missing your date," she replied in a much calmer manner than a moment ago.

It was at that moment that I glanced down at myself. Oh crap.

I was in my robe!

I put her on speakerphone as I raced back to my dresser. I set the phone on top and quickly opened drawers to grab some clothes to put on.

I had no idea where Jay lived, so I wasn't sure if he was going to be here in four minutes or forty.

"Oh, God," I said. "I just got out of the shower. When will he be here?"

"I don't know because it sounds like he's coming from the station, but put on something cute," she said, and I could hear the smile in her voice. "You should make him grovel a bit—be sure to take pictures and send them to me if you do—and then agree to go out on another date with him. Then you guys can date and eventually get married so we can become real sisters!"

She was very excited, but I was still slightly panicked that he was coming here.

"This could be so much fun, and—" she said, but I cut her off.

"Morgan, let me go so I can get ready, and I'll call you back later," I said quickly and promptly hung up the phone.

As much as I would love to chat with her, now was not the time. Apparently, now *was* the time for full-blown panic to set in.

Frozen, I stood there, naked as the day I was born in front of my dresser.

Did I go with sexy so I could rub it in his face what he missed? Did I put my pajamas on—cute ones, obviously— to pretend I didn't care?

A loud meow startled me out of my wardrobe thoughts.

I looked down to find my calico cat, Frizzle, staring at me. She had an endocrine disorder that caused her fur to look matted and have some bald patches. She may have looked a little rough most days, but she was a sweetheart.

Her appearance looked about as good as mine right now.

I decided to put on a pair of white jean shorts and a bright-pink T-shirt that said *book nerd* on the front. It was cute but not trying too hard—and most importantly, it was clean.

I pulled the towel off my wet hair and debated my options. My long, wavy hair was a lost cause due to how long it would take to dry—even in this summer heat—so up it went into a messy bun on the top of my head.

Makeup, however, could be done quickly. I slapped on some concealer and mascara just as a knock sounded on my door.

This was it.

*Breathe. You're an adult. You've got this.*

The knock came again—louder this time, like he was afraid I hadn't heard the first one.

I took a deep breath, smoothed my shirt—which I now noticed had a lot of cat hair on it—and opened the door.

Jay stood there, slightly out of breath, in a rumpled T-shirt, holding a half-squished pale-blue box and a bouquet of...daisies?

In a pickle jar?

"Cora," he blurted, eyes wide, voice slightly shaky. "I'm so sorry. I know you're probably mad, and I know you probably think I'm the world's worst date. And I am.

But I promise you I ghosted you by accident. I texted my sister instead of you."

His arm jerked as he held out the flowers and the box to me. "I'm basically a walking apology."

I snickered at his comment as I accepted the gifts. "Here. Come on in."

I watched him as he entered, taking in his wrinkled shirt and tired eyes, letting me know he came straight here instead of taking time to check how he looked.

He had an amazing body. His muscular frame had always been nice, even when we were younger, but now it was a *grown man's* muscular frame. My gaze moved to his face, showing his strong nose, sharp jawline, and a ruggedly sexy smile. Sparkling eyes that promised a good time with a mild hint of regret.

"This box is donuts from the market across the street from the station. They're not fancy, but they're damn good. And the flowers are from the flower section inside the market. They were the only ones left. I think the card says get well soon or something like that, but I'm hoping they can also say I'm sorry I'm a disaster."

I turned, moving to put the flowers on my kitchen counter beside me, as I heard my cat hiss and unhappily meow as she approached.

"You have a cat," Jay said behind me. "And judging by her demeanor, I don't think she's my biggest fan."

"Miss Frizzle is friendly, but she's just upset because you interrupted her dinnertime," I explained.

"Great...I ruined two meals for women today," he

mumbled jokingly. "Wait…Why do I recognize that name?"

"Miss Frizzle?" I asked, and he nodded. "She was the teacher in the *Magic School Bus* books."

"Oh! The cartoon TV show!" he said, putting the pieces together.

"Well, it was a book series first, but yes," I told him.

"Of course," he replied, smiling at me. "You were reading a book or holding a book almost every time I saw you."

Truth. I loved books, though. They were my escape, my dream world. The O'Haras had taken us to the library often, and sometimes I even walked there after school on my own since it was only a block away. It was my little sanctuary, and I loved it.

He paused and then added, quieter, "I've been wanting to ask you out on a date for years, and when I finally did, I blew it before we even got to breakfast."

*What did he just say? He'd been wanting to ask me out for years?*

"So, I know I don't deserve it, but if you can forgive me, I'd love to take you out to dinner on Wednesday when I have my next day off." He looked at me like he was waiting on edge for my verdict.

I stared at him, then the box of donuts in my hand, the flowers, and then back at him. His face was earnest, tired, but completely sincere.

I had already planned to give him a second chance

after I listened to his voicemail, but it made the decision that much easier when I looked into his eyes.

"Wednesday sounds great," I said, giving him a small smile.

The relief washed through him visibly, followed by a grin that was goofy, grateful, and a little sexy. "Thank you."

"Thank you for the donuts and the flowers. It was very sweet."

We both stood there for a second, quiet but on the same page, as we both smiled at each other.

"I'll let you go so you can feed Miss Frizzle," he said, looking down at her as she weaved her way around his leg, rubbing up against it.

*Lucky bitch*, I thought.

"Oh, and Cora?"

"Yeah?"

"You look...really good. Even covered in cat hair." He winked as he walked out the door, and I felt warmth coursing through my veins at his compliment.

I walked behind him to close the door and lock it, a beaming smile overtaking my face.

I was back on cloud nine and giddy as a schoolgirl.

I felt like everything was back in play, and the night was finally heading in the right direction.

# 10

## Jay

I felt a little off, and the night was already heading in the wrong direction.

I was a little nauseated. After working the last twenty-four hours and then sleeping for eight hours after that, I somehow felt worse than I had before.

My head was pounding, my stomach was unsettled, and every joint in my body ached.

I knew this was possibly—probably—the flu that had been making the rounds at work, but I told myself it was just nerves for our date since I had screwed up the first one. I should've canceled dinner with Cora, just to be safe.

Any reasonable person would have.

But I couldn't.

I'd already bailed once. Twice was unforgivable. So, I did what any idiot determined not to ruin his chances would do. I popped some meds, splashed some water on my face, and hoped for the best.

I figured I could power through a simple dinner for a few hours.

Bad decision.

Walking from my car, up the stairs to her apartment, and down the hallway to her door felt equivalent to running a 5K race, even though the real distance was probably barely fifty yards.

The second she opened her door, she smiled at me, and guilt punched me square in the chest.

I gave her my best smile as I took in the sight of her. She was wearing a sleeveless, flowy, pale-pink dress that went just below her knees. She looked stunning. I felt dizzy just looking at her beauty—although that could have been related to my previous dizzy spells.

"Are you okay?" she asked me, worry etched on her face.

"I'm good." I lied smoothly. "Just tired from a long shift."

She studied me for a second longer, likely trying to judge my sincerity, but just gave a small smile, and we made our way back to my car.

As we drove, I started a conversation to keep my mind on her instead of the medicine that still hadn't kicked in yet.

"I know some of the basics because Morgan told me,

but tell me how you went from high school tutor to badass hydrologist."

"Well, after graduating from high school, I went to college at U.C. Davis," she started to explain. "Hazel was several years younger than me, and I didn't want to move too far from her. It was just far enough from home to make me feel like I was an adult and on my own, but close enough that I could still come back home to the O'Haras for the holidays and help Hazel with prom and other big events."

I nodded, listening to everything she said, and really taking it in.

"After college, I got my first job working at the National Weather Service office in Sacramento," she continued. "Then, a few years later, I took a job at the River Flood Management Authority in Nevada."

"Forgive my ignorance, but I didn't even know such a thing existed," I said, a little embarrassed admitting that.

"It's really just a joint effort with the counties in and around Reno to figure out ways to reduce the devastating impacts of flooding. Essentially building infrastructure and managing the floodplain to reduce flood damages and create a more resilient community."

"That's cool," I replied, hoping she could see my genuine interest. "Is that how you got the job now?"

"Kind of, yes. My supervisor at that job recommended that I look into the state hydrologist job when it became available. Here I am two years later, and I have my dream job."

I couldn't contain the smile spreading wide across my face, thinking about how everything had fallen into place for her.

"What about you? How did you decide where to go for your firefighter jobs?"

"You know I was drafted right out of school—and quickly," I replied, which reminded me of the night I'd kissed her, only to bail and move away a few days later. "I moved to Texas right away to start playing and training with the team. When I was twenty-one, I was injured and immediately put on the injured reserve list."

I sighed deeply, thinking about my dream career ending sooner than I had wanted.

"Two years later, I was finally cut from the team after my injury just never allowed me to go back to playing like I had before. I knew my family wanted me to come home, but I also knew that if I did, my dad would try to get me to go to college and go into business. So, I hurried up and began training to become a firefighter and stayed in Texas."

I was happy that I'd been able to transition to my other career so easily, given that I had been injured. Even though I'd healed, being a firefighter was no joke. You had to be incredibly fit and strong for that job.

"I hated the heat in Texas, so after a couple years, I moved to Colorado and became a firefighter there," I added. "Then last year, I decided I was ready to move back closer to home. I was also ready to switch to being a fire investigator, so I moved here to finish out that goal."

"Jay, that's so awesome," she said, reaching over to touch my arm in support.

Her hand felt like fire on my skin, although maybe that was just me since I wasn't feeling a hundred percent.

"I'm so happy for you that it all worked out and you were able to become a firefighter like you always wanted."

I was surprised and happy she'd remembered, which only made me realize how much she had cared and paid attention to our conversations.

By the time we reached the restaurant, I was feeling slightly better, which made my confidence a little too high that I'd made the right decision to keep our date.

As it turned out, there was some big event in town that night, which meant the restaurant was packed. Having never been here before and knowing that it was never packed full, I hadn't thought to make a reservation. Yet another poor decision on my part.

"It will be about a thirty-minute wait." The hostess gave us an apologetic smile.

I turned to Cora to see what she wanted to do, secretly hoping maybe she would just want to reschedule for another evening and I could just take her home and sleep the rest of the night away.

"Since the venue is nearby, I'm guessing every other place is going to be just as busy," Cora said, and I knew she was likely right. "I don't mind waiting, but...you don't look like you want to stay."

I didn't want her to think I didn't want to be here with

her. I did. I just wished I felt better. Before I could answer her, though, it hit me all at once.

The unmistakable cold sweat, the certainty that I was about to throw up—immediately.

"I'll be right back," I muttered, already turning toward the bathroom before my body could betray me in public.

I barely made it in time.

I felt slightly better after getting it all out, but I knew I had to cancel. There was no powering through this. Plus, I couldn't take the chance of getting her sick, too. I just needed to explain, apologize, and hope that me at least showing up tonight counted for something.

Bracing myself, I opened the door and nearly ran straight into her. She was standing right outside the bathroom, concern written all over her face.

"Jay, seriously, you don't look so good," she said, but that was as far as she got.

Between the shock, the lingering dizziness, and my body's impeccable timing, everything went sideways. Literally.

I lurched forward, and before I could even register what was happening, I threw up again.

Right on her shoes.

And there went any hope I had of another date in the future.

# 11

## Cora

I was living the dream…one bad decision at a time.

After Jay puked on my shoes during our second attempt at a first date, I helped him get back into his car and on his way home.

He told me how he knew he wasn't feeling well, but he'd been afraid that if he'd cancelled the date, I would never give him a third chance. I understood that and even appreciated the fact that he cared so much to go through with a date when he didn't feel well at all.

I drove his truck back to my apartment, and then he insisted on driving himself home instead of taking a rideshare that I recommended. Apparently he only lived five minutes from me, so he claimed it was no big deal.

After I made him promise to text me when he got back to his place safely, I settled in for the night. I called Iris and Hazel to fill them in on what had happened, and then I called Morgan. I filled her in on everything that had happened.

"Oh my God, I am going to give him so much crap for this," she said, half laughing, half wheezing into the phone. "But as your bestie, I'm sorry this happened."

"It's okay," I told her, brushing it off as no big deal. "They were old shoes anyway."

After she finished laughing, Morgan paused as her voice turned more poetic. "So you and my brother, huh? I can't believe it's finally happening. My dream come true for you to be my real sister."

"Morgan, it's two dates, and neither of them really counts."

I knew I was playing it down out of self-preservation. Her brother had been the main character in many of my X-rated dreams, but that also meant it would break my heart if I had a chance at something with him and then lost it.

"He's always had a thing for you, Cora, and I know you liked him too," Morgan said. "Fate just took you in different directions for a while. I'm just happy it's working out now. It also makes sense now why he kept asking me a bunch of questions about you last year."

What did she just say?

"What do you mean?" I asked, trying to play my question off casually.

"He mentioned he was ready to move on from Colorado and move closer to home," Morgan explained.

"He started to ask where you lived and if you liked it here. I thought it was just because he liked Reno and wanted to know your thoughts. But now that I look back on it, I think he moved here specifically because you did."

"No, he moved here for the job, remember?" I told her, trying to downplay that possibility.

"Cora, he moved to Reno without having a job yet," she told me, and I felt my heart flutter. "I specifically remember him telling me, 'Sis, it's damn time I made the move I should have years ago.' At the time, I assumed he meant move, as in move across the country to be closer to home, but now I think he meant make a move to *you*."

A rush of feelings washed through me at her comment. Giddy disbelief, nervous excitement, and warmth filled my chest at her revelation.

I spent the rest of the night thinking—and over-thinking—about that bombshell Morgan had dropped on me.

The next day, when Jay texted to tell me he was feeling slightly better but how sorry he was and to please give him another chance Saturday night, I responded yes with a huge smile on my face.

He felt back to normal Friday when he worked his next shift and texted me all the details about making a reservation at a nice place for Saturday night and to dress up.

*I fucked up the first two dates, I'm going big for the third,* he had texted, and I'd remembered why I'd fallen for him back in high school.

He wasn't kidding. He'd made us reservations at Hormack's Steakhouse, one of the nicest restaurants in town.

I may have mildly freaked out when he told me because this stepped up the significance of the date and also meant I had to step up my wardrobe.

I was very much a pear-shaped body and was not very gifted up top, but the bottom half of me I could rock like a champ. I had a killer booty, and—thanks to being on the taller side—fantastic long legs.

I'd had this body shape my whole life and knew how to dress to flaunt my best parts. I had on a pair of high-waisted pale blue pants with a drapey V-neck navy blue sleeveless top. I also put on my slightly padded bra to give my girls a little boost.

I was wearing my hair down tonight, the way Jay liked it—or at least the way he used to. I'd also added a little bit of mousse to the ends of my hair to give my curls some volume and bounce.

The knock at my door made my heart tick up. I felt more nervous tonight than I had before the other dates. I knew they hadn't ended well, but at the beginning of each of them they all held the same amount of hope, so it seemed odd to me that I felt more anxious about this one.

Looking through the peep-hole in my door, I saw he

was wearing a tan and white linen button-down shirt with gray dress pants and a black belt. He looked delicious.

"Hey, come on in," I told him as I opened the door. "I just have to get Frizzle some water, and then we can head out."

I turned to head into the kitchen to refill her bowl and then made my way back out. He was still rooted in the same place I'd left him, just inside the doorway, though now it was closed.

"You look amazing," he said, causing my gaze to meet his, and it was then I saw the heat in them. Raw, unabashed, lustful heat filled his eyes as he scanned me up and down.

*Score one point for my awesome outfit!*

"I love your hair like that."

*Oh my gosh!*

I was so glad I remembered and had chosen to wear my hair down tonight.

The walk from my apartment to his truck felt shorter than it should have, like my nerves were skipping full speed ahead. He opened my door for me, his hand brushing my lower back just briefly enough to make my breath hitch.

By the time we pulled into the restaurant, I'd gone from confident to anxious-excessive-sweater and back again—twice.

Apparently, all it took was one sultry look from Jay to undo my carefully practiced cool-girl routine.

Walking the short distance into the restaurant—his

hand connected with mine—I replayed that look he gave me at the door at least three times.

Inside, he let go of my hand only to move it to my lower back and pull me close to his side as he gave the hostess his name for the reservation.

They exchanged words, but I couldn't tell you a single word that was said because I was too focused on the hole that was burning into my back at his touch. Tingles raced through my body at even the slightest movement of his hand. My front was pressed to his side, and I could smell his woodsy cologne all around me.

Secretly, I hoped some of it would rub off on my clothes so I could smell it long after I got home.

Shortly after we had sat down at our booth, our waiter took our drink order, and we began scanning our menus. My phone buzzed in my pocket, showing Iris calling. I knew what this call was about. I also knew that if I didn't answer, she would just keep calling.

"Sorry. Give me just a minute to get this," I told Jay apologetically as I swiped to answer the phone, accidentally putting it on speaker.

"Something very awful happened," Iris said blandly, full of sarcasm and with what sounded like a mouthful of food.

I quickly switched it off speaker and briskly walked away from the table before Iris said anything else. "Hey, Iris, it's okay. He's here and didn't ghost me or puke on me—yet," I told her.

"Yay!" she replied excitedly with her hands clapping

in the background. "So at least for date three, we're two for two, *chica*. I'm feeling good vibes."

"Yes, so far it's good," I replied. "Which is why I would like to get back to it, but thank you for calling."

"No problem," she said as I started to make my way back to Jay. "Oh, hey, really quick, before you hang up, please email me that list from your boss. You forgot."

As I made my way back to the table where Jay was seated, I was distracted because he was looking at me funny.

"What?" I asked mindlessly into the phone.

"The list of new floodplain management plans," she reminded me just as I walked up to the table. "I need it for tomorrow's meeting. Send it now, please!"

"Oh, yeah, okay. Give me fifteen minutes, and I'll get it to you," I said, planning to order my drink and food and then pull up the emails and send them to her while we waited.

I reached over to grab my jacket because it was definitely chilly in this restaurant, as my sister replied quickly before hanging up. "Thanks, love you, bye."

I set the phone down on the corner of the table and started to put my jacket on when I heard Jay mumble and move to get out of his seat.

"Wait, Cora, don't leave yet! I need to...uhh...ask you something."

I looked up to see a panicked look in his eyes.

"What?" I asked him, sliding my other arm into my jacket and then zipping it up.

"Please…ummm." He no sooner had the words out of his mouth than he dropped down to one knee on the floor and stared up at me. He grabbed my hand and pulled me closer as people around us started to stare. "Umm, Jay, what are you doing?"

"Cora, will you marry me?" His eyes widened as he asked those words loudly and quickly, like he couldn't believe he'd actually said them.

Surrounded by oohs and ahhs, I stared down at the man in front of me as though he'd sprouted a unicorn horn in the middle of his forehead.

*What did he just say?*

*What was happening right now?*

"Jay?" I whispered, trying to figure out what was going on and at the same time realizing people around us were now fully immersed in the two of us—namely me, since I hadn't responded to him.

He held up what looked to be his baseball championship ring that I'd noticed he wore on his pinky.

"Say yes, Cora," Jay said to me, loud enough for all to hear, before dropping his voice to a whisper. "Please, so everyone will stop staring."

I glanced around and saw that everyone was, in fact, still staring at us. I didn't know what to do, but I also didn't want to embarrass him. I also hated being the center of attention, and that was exactly what we were.

*Think fast.*

*Just say yes, and then badger him with questions.*

"Ummm. Yes, of course, I'll marry you." I gave the

brightest smile I could conjure up, hoping it would appease everyone around us and then I could get to the bottom of what was going on once we sat back down.

However, in my mind, I guess I just assumed he would smile, stand back up, and we would sit back down.

Nope.

He smiled, alright.

And he stood back up.

But then he put his hands on the sides of my face and kissed me.

This was no simple kiss. The instant his mouth was on mine, it consumed me, just like it had when we were in high school. It was familiar, but also deeper and heavier, as though all those years of pent-up sexual frustration were colliding all at once.

Jay released me after rocking my world, pulling back only slightly to where I could feel his breath still on my lips. "Not bad for your last first kiss."

*What did he just say?*

"Here. Have a seat," he said, taking my hand and directing me back to my seat across from him in the booth.

He never let my hand go as we both sat. The cheers and clapping around us faded, and I stared at him.

My voice was just above a whisper when I asked, "Umm...do you wanna tell me what just happened?"

"I couldn't have you leave yet." His words were simple but hardly explained anything.

"Leave yet? What are you talking about?" Before he

had a chance to respond, a tall man walked up next to our table and stuck his hand on Jay's shoulder.

"Rainer, it seems congratulations are in order," the man said, clearly knowing who Jay was.

The shock on Jay's face came back, but with a different undertone.

"Uh, Assistant Chief Leavenworth," he stuttered and then held out his hand to shake. "What are you doing here?"

"Having dinner with my wife, Clarissa." The man pointed to the woman standing behind him.

"Congratulations, you two," she said politely. "I assume you'll be bringing her to the Firefighter's Ball in a few weeks. It will be good to get to know you, dear."

She said that last part to me. I had no idea who she was or what was going on, so I just politely nodded and smiled.

"Settling down is just the right step I like to see in my top commands," Leavenworth said, jerking me out of my thoughts. "Hal and Sawyer both informed me you're high on the list for fire investigator."

"Uh, yes, sir," Jay responded.

"You coming to the meeting Monday? You should," the Leavenworth guy added.

"I'm not sure which meeting you mean, sir."

"I'll get Stetson to invite you," he said, nodding at Jay. "You should be part of it. It's virtual, so you can attend remotely while you work."

"Uh, thank you," Jay replied, a small smile on his face.

"I won't take up any more of your special night. Congratulations," he told us, and then he took his wife's hand and walked away.

"You have one chance to tell me what the hell just happened in the last five minutes before I walk out that door, Jay Rainer."

He shook his head as if to clear it before turning his full gaze on me.

"Talk," I demanded.

"You were about to leave and go meet whoever was on the phone, and I panicked," he explained apologetically and somewhat frantically.

"That was my sister, Iris. I wasn't meeting her."

He stared at me in confusion. "But you said you'd get her everything in fifteen minutes, and then you put your jacket on. You were going to meet her—and leave."

"I put my jacket on because even though it is ninety degrees outside, the inside of this restaurant is only a few degrees warmer than a freezer," I explained with a huff. "And Iris just needs me to email her some things. I told her to give me fifteen minutes because I was going to look at the menu, order my food, and then pull up the emails on my phone and send them."

His shoulders relaxed as his head dropped forward, his chin to his chest. I couldn't tell if he was relieved or upset, but then his shoulders began lightly shaking. His head turned back up, and I could see the giant smirk. He was laughing.

"Good to know you're enjoying this, while I'm over here completely confused about what just happened."

"I panicked," he said, still smiling but no longer chuckling. "I thought you were leaving, and this would be date three that didn't work out. I knew I needed to come up with something before you left me and I lost out on any chance I may have of a fourth chance."

"So you proposed?" I asked.

"In my defense, it was the first thing that came to mind," he tried to justify. "I had been fidgeting with my ring while I waited for you, so it was already in my hand."

He paused briefly in his explanation before his gaze turned more serious. "I should probably say I'm sorry, but I realize I'm actually not, at least not entirely."

He sighed and dropped his head. "And then Leavenworth and his wife showed up, and I panicked again and didn't know what to say. That man we spoke to is the key to me getting my promotion, and he makes me nervous, so the words just rolled out of my mouth before I thought better of them."

"So he's someone *really* important?" I asked.

"Yeah. That was Luke Leavenworth, the Assistant Fire Chief."

"Oh, so your boss."

"Sort of. Well, not yet. My current boss is Sawyer Stetson, my battalion chief," he elaborated. "But he reports to that man you just met. The new job I want—fire investigator—would have me report to Hal Thompson, who is the Division of Investigation Chief. He also reports to Leavenworth. So if I want this job, both of them report to him. Thompson is in charge of filling that position, but Leavenworth can ultimately pick who the role goes to."

"Who does this Leavenworth guy report to?" I asked, trying to understand the hierarchy.

"The Fire Chief, Bret Bleaker," he answered.

"Who does that man report to?"

"The mayor."

Oh shit.

This was getting more complicated by the minute, and I was afraid there might not be a way to backtrack from this.

"So what happens when that man we just met finds out the engagement was an accident and we aren't really getting married?"

"What if we don't tell anyone it was an accident and see how this goes instead?" His question was asked a bit timidly but full of hope that I would agree.

I had dreamed of being with this man since high school, and technically here was my chance. But this was not at all how I had ever envisioned this happening in my dreams.

I knew I needed to think about this—come up with my usual pros and cons list—but I couldn't do that while he was around. I needed to be at home, in my safe space, where I could let my mind analyze every detail and give myself time to process what had just happened.

I just hope this decision didn't come back to haunt me later.

# 12

## Jay

"Okay, hold on." She shook her head, sitting across from me at the restaurant. "I'm trying to remember all the names."

"Think BLTS–like the sandwich," I said very matter-of-factly. "Bleaker, Leavenworth, Thompson, and Stetson, in that order—although technically the last two are considered equals, just over different groups of people."

I felt lucky that my stupid panic moment of proposing to her ended up being perfect and could now get me *two* things I wanted—Cora *and* my promotion.

"My point is, I want that investigator role, and that man you just met is the one to help make that happen," I clarified. "It's why I was in Las Vegas two weeks ago when

I saw you and Iris. It was a favor to Thompson—the Investigation Chief and hopefully my soon-to-be new boss's boss."

"Who now thinks we're getting married," she said, putting all the pieces together.

"Did you hear what he said?" I asked because I felt like she was missing my point.

"I know his wife is excited to get to know me at some fire ball thing," she said, clearly unsure of what all that entailed.

"Yes, but Leavenworth said, 'Settling down is just the right step I'd like to see in my top commands,'" I repeated and then waited to let that sink in.

"Oh, shit," she mumbled, and I laughed at the stark change on her face.

"What's so funny?" she asked.

"I was laughing because I've never heard you swear before." That was partly the truth.

"Well, I swear a lot, so get used to it," she shot back defiantly, and it was so cute.

"You read so many books...I guess I just assumed super-smart people didn't swear," I teased.

"Or maybe I'm so smart that I realize swear words just fit the context better and voluntarily choose to use them over other words," she shot back, sticking her chin out in mock rebellion, and I felt my dick getting harder by the minute from her sassy banter.

"Come to the Firefighter's Ball with me, Cora. It's two

weeks after Morgan's wedding. Please. It would look really bad if my new fiancée didn't show up." I felt only a slight level of guilt at throwing that in at the end. If it got me my end result of having her go with me, it was worth it.

"After that, if this isn't working out between us, or it just makes you uncomfortable, then we can call the whole thing off," I offered, hoping she would accept.

While she sat there quietly, likely mulling it over in her head, I mentally started to calculate exactly how many days I had to convince her this *would,* in fact, work out between us, and I wouldn't have to break it off in the end. Hopefully.

"Okay," she replied softly, but before I could thank her, she moved right into questions. "I guess you better start telling me about this fire inspector job you want. Any good fiancée would already know all of this prior to coming to this fire ball with you."

I took in her playful grin and felt a rush of relief.

I told her everything.

I told her that since there had been so many fires set by arsonists in the last year and they weren't going away, the decision had been made to hire an additional fire inspector to help with the added caseload. I explained that I was a lieutenant and had already completed my investigator certification and training, so I was high on the list of candidates, but there was another internal option too—Trent.

"Trent was friendly in the beginning when we first

started working together, but once he found out we were aiming for the same fire investigator position, his attitude changed," I told her. "The crazy thing is, Stetson told us there is room in the budget for them to possibly hire a second position, which means there's a chance we could both get the job, so there's no reason to act like we're competition, but he does."

"I'm sorry," she said. "My co-worker Jade was kind of the same in the beginning. She wanted the job as state hydrologist, but it was given to me instead, so there was definitely some hostility in the beginning, but now that we've worked together for several months, she's really come around."

"What helped?" I asked, hoping for any advice I could possibly use.

"Umm...oddly, it was me breaking up with my ex," she explained, and I suddenly felt jealous of a man who wasn't even in her life anymore. "Spending less time with him allowed us to hang out a few more times before or after our shifts."

She filled me in on this loser guy who gave her shit about her weird schedule, and even if I hadn't been interested in Cora myself, I was glad she'd tossed this guy to the curb. He sounded like a real dick.

The check came and went too quickly, and even as we stood to leave, neither of us seemed in much of a hurry.

The ride back was filled with more catching up, and the conversation flowed easily like it had all those years ago while she tutored me or when we talked late at night on the couch after Morgan had fallen asleep. I was grateful for every red light prolonging the evening, even if for just a few moments.

By the time we pulled into her parking lot, I was running out of excuses to keep the night going, so I walked her to her door, planning to get another date on the calendar—hopefully tomorrow so I had something to look forward to.

I wanted to kiss her so badly. While we had kissed at the restaurant, I knew it was mostly for show, so I wasn't sure if she'd be willing to do it again—because she *wanted* to and not because she felt obligated. So I decided to put the ball in her court.

"Kiss me," I said, looking down at her as we stood by her door.

She paused, looking at me stoically, before a small smile crept up her face. "Okay, but I probably won't like it."

Challenge accepted.

The way my mouth took over hers, devouring her...It wasn't gentle, but it wasn't rough either. It was hungry and needy. When we finally pulled apart, breathless and with stupid grins on our faces, I knew she'd liked it more than she would ever admit.

I begrudgingly stepped away, knowing that if I didn't stop now, I'd take this too far too quickly, and I wanted to do this right with her.

"Good night, Cora," I told her, giving her a small smile.

"Good night, Jay," she said as she turned to her door and unlocked it.

Just as she was about to enter, she paused and turned back to me. "Hey Jay, I don't know anything about this Trent guy, but I know you'll get the job," she said confidently. "When you put your mind to something, you do it, and you do it well."

Fuck, this woman was good for my ego, good to look at, and good for my soul.

I was thrilled that she'd agreed to come out with me again today after I had texted her on a whim this morning.

I still needed to pick up my suit for my sister's wedding—and I was cutting it dangerously close—but I also had something special planned. Something just for her.

I told her I'd pick her up at two. That gave me two hours to run one last errand before I went to get her.

We stopped at the wedding shop first. I tried on my tux, quick and painless, but my mind was already on the rest of the day—the part I'd actually been looking forward to.

"Okay," I said as we stepped back onto the sidewalk. "First surprise."

She narrowed her eyes. "I don't like the way you said that."

I laughed. "Just trust me."

I took her hand and led her two blocks down to Windmill Park. The second we turned the corner and she saw the book festival set up across the lawn, her whole face changed. Her eyes were wide, and a smile broke free and spread across her entire face, causing me to grin like an idiot.

She moved through the booths like she belonged there. She stopped at every romance and fantasy table, chatting with vendors and flipping through books, fully in her happy space.

I wasn't a huge book guy. Give me a good mystery or thriller, and I was set, but watching her light up like that, I hadn't stopped smiling in hours.

I held her hand the entire walk back to my car. Arriving at her door, I opened it but leaned down to give her a quick kiss.

I hadn't planned it, but she just looked so damn cute with that smile stretched across her face, I needed to kiss that sweet mouth of hers again.

I would have liked to keep kissing her, but we had other plans for the day, and I had to keep going if I was going to get to the part I had been waiting for.

We didn't say much after that—just climbed into the car, still buzzing, and drove to the diner down the street to grab a bite to eat.

When I pulled into the parking lot and shut off the engine, I reached over and gently caught her arm before she could open the door.

"One more thing," I said, causing her to turn toward me curiously.

I handed her the ring I had picked out this morning. An oval-cut diamond with a white gold band to match all the other jewelry I'd noticed she wore.

For a second, she just stared at it like it might disappear if she blinked. "Jay...I...what?" She laughed nervously, shaking her head. "I don't need a real ring. Certainly not this fancy. You could've just gotten something simple. Just until...you know...all of this is over."

"Cora," I said, steady but honest. "This has to look real in every way, and there is no way I was giving you a crap ring. If I were doing this for real, this is exactly what I would've bought you."

Because I had. Standing in that jewelry store earlier today, I hadn't been pretending. I'd pictured her hand and what would look good. Admittedly, I'd also thought about her lying under me, wearing *only* that ring.

I was already rushing this from the engagement side of the relationship. I didn't want to rush her on anything else. So as much as I would love to see and touch and devour that great body of hers, I would let her set the pace for that part of this relationship.

I think even when I was younger, I knew Cora and I would end up together. My sister annoyed the hell out of me, but I wanted to hang out with her if it got me closer to Cora. After I moved away, I always asked Morgan how Cora was doing. Morgan likely thought I was just asking about her friend—and I was—but I didn't ask about any of her other friends.

In my mind, getting her a ring was inevitable. I was just ahead of schedule.

"I know, but Jay, there's no way this was cheap, and…"

I cut her off, gently sliding the ring onto her finger before she could talk herself out of it.

"People at work and at the Firefighter's Ball will notice," I said. "And if we happen to be out again for a date and someone from my work sees us, it has to be believable."

My voice dropped a little lower, but with power behind it to emphasize what I was about to tell her. "I like the idea of you wearing it. Of other guys seeing it and knowing you're not available."

Her eyebrows lifted, challenging me to explain that.

"We might not be engaged for real, but I wanna see where this goes," I told her. "I'm not done with whatever this is between us."

I pulled her closer, her hand still in mine, my other settling at the small of her back. My mouth hovered mere millimeters from hers.

"So, I guess you're going to want your fancy baseball ring back?" she asked lightly, because apparently we both needed the humor to break this up a bit.

I had given her my AAA minor league championship ring when I proposed the first time because it was all I had on me at the time.

I smiled at her. "As much as I love seeing my stuff on

you. It doesn't really send the same message." I nodded toward the diamond. "That one does."

I exhaled, the weight of everything finally catching up to me.

"Look, Cora. I fucked up," I admitted quietly. "My plan was to come home after my first year in the minors after I'd made something of myself. I wanted to prove that I had something to offer you. I was hoping to ask you to transfer schools to be closer to me."

I took a deep breath and swallowed. "Then I got hurt. There were trade rumors. Then my bigger injury. I got benched and I didn't even know if I would ever play again."

My voice dropped. "So, I kept waiting. Waiting until I was worth something again and had something to offer you. Something important enough to make you move, which was why I didn't come home right away."

She didn't interrupt me. She didn't rush to fill the silence. She just stayed there next to me, listening.

The way she looked at me then—like I wasn't a failure, like I was something worth choosing—hit me harder than the injuries ever had.

"I want this, Cora. I want this second chance so bad. If you want to, we'll tell people we're having a long engagement, that way there's no pressure," I told her, hoping that would ease her concerns a bit, and make her want it too.

"And give you time to back out," she muttered quietly, almost as if she hadn't wanted me to hear.

I put my hands on both sides of her head and pulled

her gently to me as I stared into her eyes. "Cora, I'm not going to back out."

I leaned in to close the gap and kissed her. I was going for a slow burn as I wove my hands into her hair and stretched that kiss out as long as I could.

This woman was addictive. She was a drug that had already started to burrow deep into my veins. One that smelled good, tasted even better, and I wanted nonstop.

# 13

**"My family group texts are the reason aliens haven't made contact yet. They've seen them and decided Earth isn't worth it."**
—*It's science*

## Cora

What had I gotten myself into?

I was now engaged. Sort of.

I had a ring—a real one, not just his baseball one he had given me in a panic the night before.

It was a little big, but honestly, he had guessed pretty well on my finger size. I was too afraid to get it resized, though, in case I didn't end up keeping it.

Last night I hadn't worried too much because I knew it was just something he'd done in a panic. We'd discussed that we would carry this through until just after the Firefighter's Ball so it wasn't awkward with his boss, but today that changed.

Jay made it very clear that he wanted to make a go of

this. That he was fine keeping the engagement going with no tentative end date.

*How could he be so confident?*

The logical part of my brain told me that this was all happening too fast and that I had clearly lost all sense of reason. But the dreamer in me wanted to give it a go with him, too.

In high school, I dreamed of Jay asking me to marry him and spending my life with him, but not in this exact scenario.

I needed to slow down, take a deep breath, and give my mind some time to think.

He was asking a lot for us to pretend this was real. His parents could find out. My family could find out. It was one thing to keep up the lie for just a few people, but the longer we kept this up, the more likely others would find out too. And with more people came more complications.

The consequences for me weren't nearly as big as they were for him. Being engaged clearly helped him with this new job he wanted. For me, it didn't matter. Most people at my job didn't pay enough attention to my personal life. Even if they found out I'd gotten engaged and then later called it off, most wouldn't say a word. They might look at me with sympathy, but there would be no discussion, outside of Jade.

But there were stakes when it came to my heart. I'd crushed hard on him as a teenager, only for him to break my heart when he left.

If we actually started dating, I fell in love with him,

and he broke it off down the road after he got the job and no longer needed the engagement, I wasn't sure I would recover.

Jay made me feel desired—truly wanted—in a way I had never felt with anyone else before. But that also meant if he walked away, I knew the breakup would hurt more than with anyone else before.

It was also embarrassing how much I'd thought about him over the years. Sometimes, Jay would come to my mind through seemingly innocent ways. At my first job out of college, the guy who sat at the desk next to me was a big sports buff. He talked baseball and hockey with anyone and everyone who walked by. Every time he brought up Jay's team, I found myself wanting to look up and see how he was doing. Not just in his professional life, but also in his personal one.

It was a struggle to restrain myself, and I only did it a dozen or so times—if you rounded down.

Even indirectly, he popped into my head. A few years ago, I'd gone on a date with a friend's coworker, JJ, because she thought we'd hit it off. We liked similar things and had relatable careers, but the minute he sat down and told me his real name was Jay and JJ was a nickname, all I had done on the rest of the date was think of Jay Rainer— my Jay.

My phone dinged and then dinged again in rapid succession, breaking my train of thought.

I swiped open my cell to see my family text thread was blowing up.

HAZEL:

I have great news!

ANNA:

What weird animal did you adopt now?

IRIS:

Nancy says you should adopt a man
instead.

HAZEL:

I bought a house!

MOM:

Congratulations, sweetie!

AUNTIE:

Did you have the home inspection yet? I
can help you with that if you want.

GALE:

What kind of house is it?

HAZEL:

It's a cute Craftsman bungalow. And it's
only a quarter mile from the beach.
There's a trail in the neighbor's yard I can
take to walk down to the beach!

MOM:

That's wonderful and perfect for you!

AUNTIE:

Seriously, Hazel, I know a guy who can
give you a great deal on a home
inspection. I'll go find his number and
text you.


I cringed at Auntie's comment. She always knew a guy

or gal who could fix something or do something "for a great deal." Shortly after, you realized there was a reason they never charged full price—because they never did a good enough job to *charge* full price.

I decided to shoot off my own *private* to my sister, telling her to ask her Realtor for a home inspector instead of whatever shady guy Auntie had in mind.

I also debated telling her about the engagement. It would be nice to get her advice on the subject, but I wanted to reflect on it a bit more myself because I knew she would have a million questions, and I wanted to be ready with answers. Hazel was a fly-by-the-seat-of-her-pants kind of person and could wing it in many situations. I was not. I needed to prepare, to analyze every part of a situation or project—consider all sides and their possible outcomes—and then come to a decision.

Then, and only then, would I be ready to ask Hazel, or any of my other sisters, for advice.

Until then, there was only one place I would go to for advice.

"Frizzle, what do you think we should do?" I asked, picking up my cat and snuggling her on my lap. At first, she balked at my waking her from her beauty sleep, but she quickly settled into me and allowed me to pet her while I unloaded onto her everything I was feeling.

"This is happening too fast...too soon. Right, sweetie?" I asked rhetorically as I ran my fingers through her fur. "I mean, yes, we've known each other for years...but we also haven't spoken in just as long. I mean, for all intents and purposes, he kind of came out of nowhere."

She purred in my lap, and I took that to be her agreeing with me.

"You're right. I need to play it safe, and that means slowing down and giving this time to develop naturally."

*Meow.*

"You think we should make a pros and cons list?"

I sighed, leaned back on the couch, and let my brain go to town.

"Well, the biggest pro is that we've always wanted this scenario. He's also really hot, so it wouldn't be a hardship to be in his company while this plays out. He's easy to talk to, fun to hang out with, and he pays attention to details," I said, thinking back on the pop-up book fair he'd taken me to earlier today.

"The biggest con is obviously that he could break our hearts," I said, my heart pinching at the thought of it.

"Okay, we need to decide," I told her. "Meow once if you think we should go for it, or hop off my lap if you think we should walk away before we get hurt."

She just stared up at me as though she thought *I* was the idiot in this scenario.

"Nothing? Really? No advice whatsoever to the person who feeds you and keeps you alive?"

*Meow.*

Was that her response to my previous question or my new one?

"Ugh," I groaned and then sighed.

Another ping of text came through from my sister.

HAZEL:

LOL. Don't worry, I hadn't planned on
using anyone Auntie recommended.

ME:

Good. I can't wait to see your new place!

HAZEL:

Thanks. I just needed to finally make the
move. Take the big risk.

HAZEL:

I'm really happy I did.

There it was. That was the sign I needed.

Take the chance.

I knew she was talking about her house, but I was taking it as a sign to let this thing with Jay play out and trust that if it was meant to be, then it would be.

# 14

**"The more important the meeting, the more likely you are to spill something all over yourself."**
—*It's science*

## Jay

"Rainer! Get in here!" my battalion chief, Stetson, called out from his office shortly after I came into work Monday.

As I hit the threshold of his door, I noticed Stetson, Trent, and Chief Thompson sitting at the square table, and they had a Zoom call pulled up on the big TV on the wall.

"Leavenworth said I should get both of you on this call since you're both applying for the open inspector position," Stetson said, waving his arm for me to have a seat.

Stetson's and Thompson's attitudes were neutral, but Trent was clearly unhappy that I was also invited, which was ridiculous since we both knew the other had applied for the position.

"Thank you all for joining," Leavenworth said to begin

the meeting. "First, congratulations are in order for one of our colleagues."

My heart started racing because I had a feeling he was talking about me, and I knew that would bring up more questions for Stetson and Trent since I hadn't had a chance to tell them.

"My wife and I were out to eat Saturday and happened to witness Lieutenant Rainer propose to his girlfriend, and she said yes," Leavenworth announced, followed by clapping and cheers of congratulations from everyone on the call.

Everyone except Trent, who mumbled, "Congratulations," though there was no sincerity to it.

Stetson also had a curious look on his face but slapped me on the shoulder and still gave me a genuine congratulations.

"Happy to see him settling down," Leavenworth said. "And she only seemed mildly scared at the prospect of marrying him."

A round of laughs ensued, but my only thought was, *If only he knew.*

"Alright. Now to the real reason we're all here," Leavenworth spoke again, a more serious and direct tone. "We had another arson in the past week. This one killed a couple who were camping nearby."

A round of curses could be heard both in the room I was in and from other people on the call.

"Are there any signs of escalation with the arsonist?" Chief Bleaker asked.

"All the fires so far with the same pattern—the ones we believe to be connected—have all been in forestry areas or abandoned warehouses," Thompson replied. "So, it appears the victims were not targeted but just happened to be in the wrong place at the wrong time."

Our first fatal fire had been two drug dealers who were trying to store their supply inside a cave they found in a forest that caught fire. The police initially suspected it was a rival drug gang that set the fire. But a few weeks later, another fire was set with the same accelerant pattern.

This person knew about fire. They knew what accelerants worked best to achieve their goal of spreading rapidly.

The second fatal fire had been a homeless person who was sleeping in their car in a parking lot near a wooded area. That fire was what caught the attention of the forestry service and our local fire officials because everything about that second fire looked like it had been a planned controlled burn—except no one knew about it.

Wind had also taken those flames farther north, near the parking lot where the man had been sleeping.

This meant that while the person had some knowledge about wildfires, they hadn't had much knowledge about the impacts of weather on the fires. It was why Bleaker had requested the National Weather Service and a forensic meteorologist get involved to assist with the investigation.

After going over more details of what the investigations had come up with, Bleaker gave everyone commands so he could report back to the mayor's office on what we were doing in order to ease the public's concern.

"Thompson...take Tannin and Rainer with you when you meet with BAER and the other teams tomorrow," Bleaker told him regarding Trent and me. "Stetson, Leavenworth can arrange to give you some other firefighters tomorrow to fill their vacancies while they're out in the field."

As soon as the call ended, Trent turned to me. "Did you knock some girl up? What's with the quickie engagement to a woman we didn't even know you were dating?"

"Tannin!" Stetson growled his disapproval at Trent's accusation.

I understood Trent's skepticism because most of the people who worked here were family, so we often brought our spouses or partners around.

"Cora is my sister's best friend. I've known her for years, but we just recently re-connected after I moved here." I hoped that explanation would be enough for now.

"Congrats, Rainer," Thompson said. "I'm assuming you'll be bringing her to the ball in a few weeks?"

"Yes, sir."

"Good. I look forward to meeting her," he said to me and then turned to position himself between Trent and me. "Both of you, be here at eight hundred hours sharp tomorrow so we can head to the scene of the arson to meet with the crews."

"Will do, sir," I replied, followed by Trent's echo.

"Alright you two," Stetson interrupted. "Get out of my office and get back to work."

Trent and I walked out of his office. We were only a few steps out into the hallway before Trent whispered to me, "I don't know what kind of shit you're trying to pull with this bullshit engagement, but if you did it to score some points with Leavenworth and Thompson, it's pointless. They'll see right through your bullshit, just like I do."

He didn't give me a chance to say anything before he stormed off down the hall, muttering curses the entire way.

I was about to follow him, but my phone started buzzing. I glanced down to see my mom's name on the screen.

> MOM:
>
> I know you might be busy at work, but please call me as soon as you can!
>
> MOM:
>
> Not an emergency per se, but you need to call me.

The hairs on my neck started to stand up because my mom knew I worked weird hours and never sent messages like that unless it was important.

Before I could let myself freak out about whether something had happened to her or my dad, I texted her back while putting some of our tools back in the ladder truck.

ME:

Is everything okay?

MOM:

You tell me.

That wasn't cryptic at all.

ME:

I'm fine. I'm in the middle of checking some equipment. Can I call you in about 15 minutes?

MOM:

That's fine. But don't forget, because it's kind of weird when people keep coming up to me congratulating me on my son getting engaged, and I didn't even know he was dating anyone.

Oh shit.

As much as I needed to talk to her, I needed to talk with Trent first. I walked out into the kitchen and then the common area to find him, but no luck. After a few minutes of searching, I found him in the weight room with Nate and Blake, two of the other firefighters in our battalion.

"Hey Tannin, you got a minute?" I asked, not wanting to have this conversation—one that was already contentious—in front of the others.

"No," he replied curtly.

"Trent, I was hoping..." I started to say, but he cut me off.

"This crap you're trying to pull to steal this job from me is bullshit, and you know it, Rainer," Trent shot back.

"You guys, why don't—" Blake tried to interrupt.

Ignoring him, Trent lowered his voice, not in volume, but in tone, and continued. "There's nothing about the arsons that's a mystery to me. I know the ins and outs of every single one of these fires. There is no way you're going to beat me when it comes to figuring this case out, and you know it, so you had to pull this stunt."

"I'm not trying to beat you, dude," I responded, shaking my head. "We're a team. As long as the team solves the case, that's all that matters."

"Maybe that's how it works once you're on the team, but we aren't, so this is absolutely a competition. One where I'm going to win and you're going to lose."

"What crawled up your ass, Tannin?" Nate said as he walked by. His voice was friendly, but you could tell he wasn't thrilled with what he'd heard Trent say.

"Stay out of it," Trent shot back tersely. "This doesn't concern you."

"Like hell it doesn't," Nate replied, friendliness now gone from his voice. "We're part of the same crew, and we need to have each other's backs. We rely on each other in the field. Cohesion means safety and trust. Without it, it makes doing our job harder, so fuck yes, it concerns me."

"Trent, leave it alone," Blake added. "Why don't you go wash that big fancy truck you just got a few weeks ago, and stop trying to start shit."

"Everything all right?" Nicole Spice, our EMS Chief, said as she walked up, likely hearing the commotion.

"Did you hear Rainer got engaged?" Trent announced to everyone. "That's right, the man who hasn't been on a date since he got here suddenly has a fiancée. A fiancée, I might add, who now makes him look like the perfect candidate to Leavenworth for the job we're both competing for."

"Why would that matter?" Blake asked.

"Leavenworth said he was happy to see him settling down," Trent argued.

"Just because he didn't tell us about his dating life doesn't mean he was single," Nate pointed out. "Spurman separated from his wife and was practically signing divorce papers before any of us knew."

"That's because that's bad news," Trent shot back, and I knew what he meant. "Getting engaged is good news. News you would *think* he would want to share with us— that is…if it's actually true."

"You think he got catfished?" Blake chimed in.

"No, I think he made the whole thing up," Trent said to Blake, though his gaze was on me as he said it. "Probably just hired a prostitute long enough to secure the job."

I knew he didn't know her, but just the thought of him calling Cora a prostitute—and after the last few interactions I'd had with him, I wouldn't put it past him to say that to her face—had me seeing red.

I was about to fire off a warning to him, but Nicole beat me to it.

"That's enough, Trent," Nicole shot out. "Go outside and cool off." Her voice was in full boss-mode, letting him know without a doubt this conversation was done.

Except Trent wasn't ready for it to be finished.

"Oh, you sucking his dick too, Spicy?" Trent shot at Nicole. "Mine's bigger. Why don't you try a real man?"

"First," Nicole said, turning to him, her demeanor changing 180-degrees to pissed off. "It is highly inappropriate for you to speak to me that way not only as a woman, but also as your superior. Second, I don't suck dick because I don't swing that way. But even if I did, I feel confident both of you would be highly disappointing in that department."

The few other people who had now gathered in the room laughed.

"Tannin. My office. Now!" Stetson yelled from the doorway, looking very displeased.

"Sir?" Trent replied, easing the anger in his voice slightly, clearly realizing he had crossed the line.

"That's an order," Stetson decreed from the doorway before disappearing down the hall.

"And take your small dick energy with you," Nicole mumbled, but I still heard it.

"This isn't over." There was so much anger in Trent's eyes as he said those words. He was fuming as he stormed out of the room.

That hadn't gone well at all.

I also had a feeling Trent was about to get written up for his comments to Nicole, if not potentially fired.

"On a lighter note, I guess congratulations are in order," Nate said from the other side of the room, clearly trying to diffuse the intensity in the room.

"I'm not sure if we should congratulate her when we finally meet her, or warn her about all your weirdness," Nicole teased.

That was the thing. We all gave each other shit, but it was all in fun. Trent's comments hadn't been in fun. They'd been filled with hate and anger.

"Ha-ha," I said slowly, rolling my eyes at them and adding a little swagger to my step as I walked closer to them. "Her name is Cora, and saying yes to me was the best decision she ever made."

Cora may not agree with that statement now, but I would make it so that she absolutely believed it in the coming weeks. I just needed to convince her.

Which reminded me about my mom's message. I grabbed my phone and called her back.

That led to a ten-minute conversation that I thought I handled well and ended on a good note, but now came the hard part.

Calling Cora and giving her a heads-up. Because I knew my mom, and that meant we had very little time before the entire town knew.

As much as I would have rather called her, I knew she was working, and I also needed to get back to work, so I opted for a text, hoping I could fill her in on all the finer details later.

ME:

So don't get mad…

CORA:

Says every man on the planet before they tell you something you will get mad about…

ME:

This one isn't entirely my fault.

CORA:

What did you do?

ME:

Apparently my parents' neighbor was at the restaurant Saturday night and saw us get engaged. She just saw my mother at the grocery store and congratulated her. Which prompted my mom to call me.

Her responses so far had been quick. But her next reply took quite a bit longer to come in.

CORA:

What did you tell her?

ME:

The same thing we've told everyone else. We're engaged. We can't back down now and risk someone finding out. Look how quickly this has spread already, and my parents live more than three hundred miles away.

The dots appeared and disappeared multiple times, and I wondered what was going through her mind. Probably some mild panic, but hopefully not enough to call this whole thing off. I took that opportunity to give her something to calm her down, hopefully.

ME:

I told her we hadn't told your family yet so not to tell anyone just yet.

CORA:

Your mom can't keep a secret to save her life.

Damn, sometimes it sucked that she knew my mom so well.

ME:

Yes, but I may or may not have threatened her that we would elope in Vegas without any family in attendance if she blew the secret.

CORA:

Jay!!!! Now she's going to hate me!

ME:

Nah. She already loves you.

ME:

Look, I have to get back to work, but I'll fill you in tonight. I promise it's not bad. She was very excited. I just wanted you to know in case my mom calls you.

CORA:

You told her not to tell anyone…Why
would she call me?

ME:

Exactly for that reason. She can't tell
anyone new. Which means she could
call you, since you already know and
she's likely dying to tell someone.

She didn't respond. Not after I sent that message. Not an hour later when I rechecked my phone. Not even five hours later when I had another chance to check my phone.

I had a feeling I was in for a late-night phone call of groveling with Cora.

Good. Hopefully this would give me some practice, since I would likely be groveling to her a lot over the next few decades as husband and wife.

# 15

## Cora

Holy heatstroke from hell, it was hot outside. I was pretty sure I already had a sunburn, even though I'd only been outside for sixty seconds.

That might have been a stretch. Then again, maybe not.

I was at the scene of yet another fire. This one, unfortunately, had killed two campers who'd been unable to evacuate in time. The air still carried the mixed smell of charred earth and ash, even though the flames had been long extinguished.

Jade had come out to assist again today, mostly because this was a large fire and it would take hours to canvas the area. I was in my element here—calm and methodical. I could turn this entire disaster area into a data set, but photography was not my forte, so Jade took over those responsibilities. She was big into photography, so I knew this was right up her alley.

As if it being a sauna outside wasn't punishment enough, I recognized several of the BAER members as we approached—one in particular who made my stomach turn.

Darren.

Of course, he was here.

Apparently, the universe had decided that potential heatstroke alone wasn't enough suffering for one day.

He stood a short distance away, hands planted on his hips as he surveyed the charred remains of the trees. His posture screamed "angry nature warrior," and I fought the urge to roll my eyes.

"I hate seeing these trees destroyed," Darren muttered as he looked around. "Sequoias are highly endangered."

Jade nodded in agreement. "Yes, but at least the seeds in the pinecones survived. Hopefully, in the years to come, we'll get a bunch of new beautiful trees. Sequoias are known for having their seeds released through their pinecones when temperatures get really hot."

Jade was right, and she was also sympathetic to Darren's somber mood. I was happy she was the optimistic type of person she was to help bring a positive spin on a bleak event like this.

"You're so right," Darren said, turning toward her with that smile I used to think was charming. "And so smart."

I internally cringed.

How had I ever found him attractive? Listening to him flirt with my coworker made him sound so much more performative and showier than I ever remembered. Maybe he'd always been that way, and I just hadn't wanted to see it.

"Are you going to come with me to take photos?" Darren asked, glancing at Jade and me.

I couldn't think of anything I wanted to do less.

"I'm on photography duty!" Jade chimed in brightly before I could answer. "I left the camera strap in the car. I'll be right back."

She practically skipped away, blissfully unconcerned that she'd just left me in isolation with my ex.

"Cora," Darren began, lowering his voice like we were about to share a special moment. "I just wanted you to know that I'm seeing someone new."

I stared blankly at him.

*What exactly did he expect from me? Tears? Regret? Maybe some applause?*

"Umm…congratulations?" I offered weakly.

Yeah, apparently that was the best I could come up with.

He stepped closer. Too close. His hand landed on my shoulder.

"I know you were in love with me and the breakup was hard."

*Say what?*

His fingers began tracing slow circles along my shoulder and then sliding down toward my back.

*Oh, hell no.*

I was just about to step away when a familiar deep voice cut through the space behind me—calm, controlled, but unmistakably furious.

"You have two seconds to take your hand off my fiancée, or I'll do it for you." Jay's menacing voice was crystal clear and caused Darren's body to jolt like he'd been electrocuted.

The second he let go, Jay stepped in, wrapping his arm around my waist and pulling me flush against him. He was solid and steady. A wall of muscle and restrained violence at my back.

Darren blinked up at him. "Your what?"

*What was Jay doing here?*

"I'm her fiancé," Jay replied evenly. "And you shouldn't put your hands on someone without permission, especially when you don't know them."

I knew exactly what was going to come out of Darren's mouth next, but I wasn't quick enough to stop him.

"I do know her," Darren shot back. "Quite well, actually. *Intimately.*"

That last word was said low and slow to make his point.

It was at that very moment that I wished the earth would just swallow me whole. Alas, it was just not my day today.

Jay didn't respond right away. But I felt it—the tension coiling through him and the rigidness of his body.

"Well," Jay said at last, his voice low and deliberate.

"Now I'm the one who knows her quite well...and intimately. So, you will refrain from touching her again."

His words rolled out like thunder as he made his point to Darren.

"Everything okay here?" a man I didn't recognize asked as he approached.

"All good now, Trent," Jay replied without looking away from Darren. "I was just explaining to this man that he needed to remove his hands from my fiancée."

*Trent. So this was the guy who was in the running for the same job as Jay.*

Trent's expression morphed as he assessed the situation. It wasn't openly hostile, but it wasn't friendly either. It was best described as sharp and calculated. What I couldn't tell was whether the shift was meant for Darren or Jay.

"So, you are the lucky woman we've heard nothing about," he said to me, curiosity clearly piqued. "Congratulations to both of you on your fast engagement."

The words were polite, but the tone was not.

"Oh! Is this your fiancé, Cora?" Jade's voice chirped as she returned, camera strap now secured around her neck. "I'm Jade. It's so nice to meet you. You should come by the office sometime and meet the rest of Cora's coworkers."

I closed my eyes briefly.

"So...you aren't the only one keeping secrets," Trent added lightly, glancing between Jay and me.

"Oh, I think it's very romantic that they got engaged so quick," Jade chimed in a super sweet voice, completely unaware of the fire she was fanning. "Especially since they hadn't seen each other in years. They just met up… and boom…they got engaged!"

Oh God. I felt panic beginning to creep up my spine.

Despite her chipper voice, I knew how her explanation sounded, especially to someone who already appeared suspicious.

At work, I'd kept the explanation simple when coworkers noticed the ring on my finger. Jay had been my high school crush. He'd moved here, and we'd reconnected. End of story. It would make the potential eventual breakup easier.

I hadn't considered how that simple story might seem to someone like Jade and others.

My gaze moved to Trent. He was now studying Jay with an intensity that could have scorched the Earth. Jay had said Trent was competitive about the job, but I didn't understand the wickedness that seemed to be raging on his face.

"So, this is the lucky lady, eh?" another man said as he stepped up beside Jay.

"Yes, sir. This is my fiancée, Cora," Jay introduced immediately. "Cora, this is Hal Thompson—Division Chief of Investigations."

Ah, the T in the BLTS sandwich of hierarchy at the fire department.

"It's a pleasure to meet you, Mr. Thompson."

"I didn't know you worked with BAER Teams," he said to me.

"Oh, technically I don't. I'm actually a hydrologist with the state," I clarified. "I work closely with the National Weather Service and am here to do burn scar and soil assessments. This is my colleague, Jade."

"Wonderful. Glad to have you both," Thompson said with a nod before turning back to Jay and Trent. "Let's go grab some equipment from the truck and get moving to the western side."

"I'll be right over, sir," Jay told him, and he nodded and walked off, as did most of the others, giving us a brief moment alone.

"What are you doing here?" I asked him. "Did you get the promotion already?"

"No. I was asked to come shadow today so that we could see what a real-life investigation assessment was like and to maybe offer some help since these arsons seem to be ticking up in frequency."

I nodded, knowing he was right.

Jay used his arm, which was still around my waist, to pull me in slightly closer as he leaned in to whisper in my ear. "I'll call you later. But do me a favor and stay away from Darren. I don't trust him around you."

"Okay," I replied, rolling my eyes at this small show of jealousy.

He moved his lips to meet mine in a quick but firm kiss. "See you later, sweetheart."

He smiled at me, and for once, it seemed genuine instead of arrogant or cocky.

"He's cute. You should definitely keep him," Jade chimed in from a few steps behind me, breaking me out of the stupor Jay had put me in. "I'm going to start taking pictures on the far side with Darren. I'll meet you back here."

"That sounds great, thanks," I told her, though I stayed rooted to my spot for a few more minutes, wondering what kind of trouble I had gotten myself into.

It was one thing to pretend for a few people that Jay and I were together, but news of our "engagement" was spreading like wildfire—which was only going to make it harder to explain in the long run.

Plus, the more he kissed me and touched me—to make it look real for the others—the harder I knew it would be for me if he broke it off.

I hadn't really panicked about Mrs. Rainer until I got home and had time to relax enough to really think about what Jay had said.

Oh, God. Mrs. Rainer thought we were engaged! Which meant the whole town probably knew by now.

*Don't panic. Breathe.*

Jay had called me on my way home since he'd ended up having to stay late, and he'd given me the full rundown of exactly how the phone call with his mom had gone.

As he explained, I realized I was happy he wasn't here so he couldn't see my face.

"I told her the same story we've told everyone else," he said very nonchalantly.

"Jay," I grumbled, because this was now starting to get out of control.

"Cora, stop worrying. She's happy about it and even told me this was one of the best decisions I'd made with my life."

I smiled a little at his mom's kind words. It wasn't that I didn't want to be with Jay, but what would we do if we broke this off? I didn't want his parents to hate me or think less of me.

"It's just…I'm worried about what they'll think when—" I started, but he cut me off.

"I told her there was no one else I would rather spend my life with, and we were happy, but to please not share with anyone else until we had the chance to tell your family."

"Thanks," I grumbled, hating the way my heart beat a little faster at his compliment and also still a little peeved at him for not telling his mom the truth and putting us in this situation. "How much time do you think that gives me before the whole town knows?"

He chuckled conspiratorially. "I'm guessing she told my dad immediately because she can't not tell someone, but she knows my dad will keep his mouth shut. My guess is…you've got two days max before she tells Morgan, who will then tell the whole damn town."

I groaned because I loved my best friend, but I knew she

*was terrible at keeping secrets. I made a mental note to call her tomorrow and explain the situation to her. And also call Hazel and tell her so I could get her advice on what to do about this whole mess.*

I had just fed Miss Frizzle and was sitting on the couch trying to relax from my crazy day when my phone rang. I glanced down at the screen to see Morgan's name. Did she already know? Or was this about her own wedding and unrelated?

"Hello," I answered cautiously.

"Umm...so our old neighbor called Mom yesterday to tell her she saw you and Jay at a restaurant Saturday, and you got engaged. I assumed she was confused, but then Mom said she talked to Jay and he said it's true. Cora?" Morgan rattled all that off without taking a breath, and I didn't know what to say.

Annnnnd Mrs. Rainer's phone tree had already started making its rounds.

I knew Morgan might be mad if I hadn't told her, but she was also my best friend, so I didn't want to lie either.

"Morgan, if I tell you what really happened, you have to pinky promise on your grandma's life that you won't tell a soul," I explained. "Not your soon-to-be hubby, not your parents, not even your dog!"

"Oh shit, this is gonna be good," she said, and I heard rustling in the background. "Okay, I'm in a safe space. Pinky promise. Tell me *everything*."

And I did.

I told her all of it in great detail.

"So now you understand why we have to keep it going," I justified.

"For how long?" she asked, and it was a question I had asked myself many times in the last few days.

"Umm...well...I don't actually know. Jay didn't clarify that."

Her response was to just laugh into the phone. "Bestie, I'm only telling you this because I love you more than him, but he's not gonna let you go. He's wanted you for a long time and now he has you. He's going to find any way to keep you, and I hope he does, because then—"

"Then we can be sisters," I finished for her. "Yeah, I know. But...this is just weird."

"What part is weird?"

"Truthfully, the whole thing," I told her and then paused. "I just don't know what to do."

"Bestie, I know this is my brother, and yes, this is my dream come true for you two to be together—even though anyone *being* with my brother grosses me out—but if I honestly thought he was a dick or would treat you badly in any way, I would tell you. And I would also do anything I could to get you out of this. But I know he loves you, and I know you love him too. Circumstances that were out of both of your control just delayed the timing for you. But now it's here, and I think you should take the leap of faith and...jump."

Morgan was right. I looked back at my life and Jay's and what each of us had done in the years since high school.

I was so happy with how my life had turned out career-wise thus far. Jay had mentioned a few days ago that he had wanted me to follow him to Texas and go to school there after he got settled, but I wasn't sure I would have.

I had never been happier with my career, and it sounded like Jay's life had turned out pretty good too.

It was that thought that made me realize if I had followed Jay around the country right after high school so he could follow his dreams, I may not have been able to achieve mine.

Maybe the timing just wasn't meant to be for us to be together early on...but now?

I had a feeling that now the timing was just right.

# 16

**"Rainfall is measured in inches and millimeters.
My emotions are measured in pints of ice cream."**
*—It's science*

## Cora

A week had passed, and while Jay and I had talked every night, tonight was the first opportunity we'd had to go on a date due to our crazy schedules.

In some ways, it felt like we had just picked up where we'd left off in high school in terms of conversation and familiarity. But there was definitely something new, something deeper, that threaded through our relationships and still brought butterflies to my stomach.

Like right now, as my stomach fluttered at just the simple touch of his hand on my thigh as he drove his truck out of my complex.

My phone buzzed. I glanced down at the screen and saw Morgan's name. "It's your sister. Let me pick up in case it's important."

Jay chuckled. "It probably isn't, but go ahead."

I had barely even gotten my hello out before Morgan launched straight in. "Wedding emergency! I have a huuuuuuuuuge favor to ask. I need six more picture frame vases for my centerpieces, but all the craft stores here are sold out, and they won't make it here in time with shipping. But your store has ten of them. Can you swing by and get them for me?"

She spoke so fast that it was a wonder I understood anything she'd said. "Yes. Text me what they look like, and I'll grab them tonight."

"This is why you are the bestest best friend *ever!*" she replied, shrieking at the end, which I knew Jay heard, based on the way he rolled his eyes as I said goodbye and then hung up the phone.

Jay raised an eyebrow at me. "Real crisis or wedding crisis?"

"Neither…It was actually a wedding *emergency*," I replied, using Morgan's words and smiling.

We had just pulled up to the restaurant when my phone buzzed a second time.

Jay laughed before I even looked at the screen.

"Yes, Morgan," I answered, confirming his likely suspicion.

"The flowers," she replied immediately, her voice laced with concern. "What if the florist can't get my peonies in time? I need a backup plan."

I pinched the bridge of my nose. "Morgan. Breathe. Your florist likely has a backup plan of her own. Trust her.

If not, your wedding planner will know what to do. Everything will be fine."

"You're right. You're right. Okay. I'm fine."

We hung up again with the promise of chatting tomorrow.

"She good now?" Jay asked as he parked and turned off the engine.

"She's one Google search away from a full-blown crisis, but for now, I think she's okay."

Jay came around to open my door, and just as I was getting down from his truck, my phone rang for the third time.

I didn't even have to look at the screen. Jay swiped to answer the call and hit the speaker button. Morgan had no sooner started to speak than Jay cut her off.

"Morgan, your wedding will be fine. Stop panicking and call your wedding planner if you have questions."

"Wait, who... Jay? Is that you?" she demanded to know but didn't wait for a response. "Why is he...Oooooh. Oh, God, Cora. You're on a date!"

That last word finished on a squeal.

"Yes, Morgan," I said, heat climbing up my cheeks. "I'm on a date."

"With my brother?" she asked, clearly hopeful that what she'd heard wasn't just a dream.

"Yes, she's on a date with your brother, who would like to actually finish the date," Jay teased.

"Well, don't finish too quickly, Jay. Women don't like that," Morgan said and then made a choking sound. "Oh

God. I think I just threw up a little in my mouth at that thought."

Jay rolled his eyes as I chuckled.

"Okay. I'm hanging up. We'll talk later!" She disconnected before I could respond.

"Turn your phone to silent—or better yet...turn it off entirely." Jay tilted his head, eyeing my phone. "I don't trust her not to call back four more times."

My chuckle now became a full-blown laugh. "She's not that bad."

"I would stand here and argue with you about the level of annoyingness of my sister, but I'd like to eat before the end of the century, so let's just go inside." He put his hand on the small of my back and guided me to the front door.

We'd picked a casual restaurant only five minutes away since we were both hungry but too tired to get dressed up or go too far from my apartment.

Dinner was easy. Comfortable. We talked about family and old memories—like the time Morgan had tried to ride one of our llamas, Bob, on the farm and ended up being chased by him as she screamed bloody murder across the pasture.

He laughed so hard that he nearly knocked over his drink. "Oh my God...I can't wait to tease her about that."

At one point, he reached across the table and stole one of my fries, just like he used to in high school.

"You never learned," I said, remembering how I used to threaten to jump him if he did that.

"Maybe this time, I *want* you to jump me," he said and then winked at me as he ate the fry with a sly grin plastered to his face.

Later, as we waited for the check, he leaned back in his chair and studied me in that quiet way he used to when I would tutor him.

"I didn't think I'd get this," he muttered softly.

"Get what?"

"Another shot."

Something heavy settled in my chest. He reached across the table and took my hand in his as he stroked his thumb over the back of my hand. Those butterflies from earlier came rushing back in with a vengeance.

He walked me to his truck after and gave me a small kiss on my lips.

"Thank you for giving me this second chance," he whispered and then placed another soft kiss on my forehead before driving me back to my apartment.

The short ride felt even quicker than usual. He parked and turned toward me.

"I'd invite you in," I told him and then added a smirk. "But I'm just going to go in, grab my keys, and run over to grab these emergency vases for the wedding."

"That's fine," he said, leaning over into my space. "I just need some emergency kisses first."

His lips brushed mine, softly at first, warm and unhurried. I caught the faint taste of beer and cheeseburger as he deepened the kiss, and then he slid his hand up to cup my jaw and draw me closer.

When he finally pulled back, he rested his forehead against mine as we tried to steady our heavy breathing.

"I could come with you," he offered. "I've never picked out emergency vases before, but I could keep you company."

"More like keep me distracted," I said, and that was exactly what he would be—a distraction.

"Cora, did you just say that I am so ruggedly handsome that you would be distracted by my devilish good looks the entire time we were together?"

His teasing nature had me wanting to tease right back. "That's not at all what I said."

"But it's what you were thinking," he goaded, trying to bait me into saying yes.

He *was* correct, but I'd never tell him that.

"You better go before I follow you upstairs and we find something else to do with our time instead of getting wedding vases." The heat in his eyes as his low voice made that declaration was enough to set my panties on fire.

His idea sounded like a much better time. Alas, I had bestie responsibilities to handle. I pulled my head back and looked at him, imagining all the things he might do to me if we went upstairs instead.

"Cora, don't look at me like that if you want to make it to the vase store," he grumbled.

I licked my lips before correcting him. "It's a craft store."

"Go," he ordered. "Call me when you get back, and we can FaceTime."

We'd done that a few other times in the past few days, and I'd loved it.

An hour later, I called him to show him the supplies I had gotten for the wedding, and he sat on his couch and pretended to care about all of it, even though I knew the details of the wedding made no difference to him at all.

He shifted on the couch, and something caught my eye as he turned.

"What... What is that on your table?" I asked, squinting to see better.

It looked like a statue of a man, but with plants.

"Huh?" He turned his head toward the table to see what I was referring to and then started to laugh. "Oh, that's my lazy guy planter."

The confused look on my face must have said more than words ever could.

"It's a pot that looks like a statue of a man with one pot on his head for hair, and another small pot between his legs, where I put a cactus so it looks like a dick." He pointed at the respective pot as he spoke with a grin.

Yep... That was exactly what I'd thought and exactly what it looked like.

"The guys at the firehouse got it for me for my birthday," he said, grinning from ear to ear.

"What a...umm...lovely gift," I said, trying to keep a straight face.

"I'd been thinking about getting a pet, but a wise woman once told me that I should start with a cactus," he said, and memories of our tutoring conversations flooded me.

He remembered.

"I asked Blake because he's actually really good at gardening and shit, and the next thing I knew the guys bought me the pot and the plants to go in it with a note that said 'Happy Birthday. Don't fuck this up.'"

We both laughed, but I also couldn't help smiling at the fact that he remembered a single conversation from so long ago.

We then went on to chat about anything and everything under the sun. Just like all the other times we'd done this, time flew by, and after two hours of chatting, I was exhausted.

"Okay, it's time for me to head to bed. I need to get my pajamas on," I told him.

"You can do that on FaceTime. I don't mind." A greedy, wicked smirk played about his face.

I chuckled a little and shook my head. "*Goodnight, Jay.*"

He sighed dramatically. "Fine. I'll just have to use my imagination. Goodnight, Cora."

We hung up, and I thought about him using his imagination to picture me. I smiled, wondering what he would do with that knowledge.

I kept smiling as I brushed my teeth, changed, and climbed into bed. Then I fell asleep using my own imagination of what Jay would look like getting undressed and into his pajamas.

I slept well. And had even better dreams.

I woke to the sound of my phone buzzing incessantly. After a few moments, I reached over to see that the text thread with my sisters was blowing up.

> HAZEL:
>
> Nigel just threw a scallop at me.
>
> ANNA:
>
> Who is Nigel?
>
> HAZEL:
>
> Our new octopus.
>
> IRIS:
>
> What did you do to him?
>
> HAZEL:
>
> Nothing!
>
> ANNA:
>
> How does an octopus throw something
> at you?
>
> GALE:
>
> Octopuses exhibit object-throwing
> behavior when they are displeased or
> not cognitively stimulated.
>
> IRIS:
>
> That's science for "he hates you."

HAZEL:

I already fed him and gave him a toy to
play with. He's just being an asshole.

ME:

On the bright side, scallops are soft, so
at least you didn't get hurt.

GALE:

Actually, that's just the part you eat. It's
probably still in its shell in the exhibit.

HAZEL:

It is. The soft part is on the inside… He
threw the whole shell at me. It was
definitely hard and also cut the side of
my forehead.

ANNA:

Just recapping… An octopus threw a
seashell at you…hit you in the head…
and cut your face? Did I read that right?

IRIS:

LOL I needed this convo today.

I was with Iris. I loved my sister, but this was hilarious.

I missed all of them and wished we lived closer. The biggest problem was that we all worked jobs that operated 365 days a year—except Gale. But Gale still helped out on the family farm, which *was* a year-round job itself, so it was hard for all of us to sync our schedules, even for holidays.

Chatting with them calmed me, centered me in a way that made me feel good from the inside out. And I needed that goodness. Tomorrow we were leaving for the wedding, and I was so nervous.

I decided I could use this time to ask for some advice. Plus, this conversation definitely needed a topic change.

ME:

I need help.

HAZEL:

Is this regarding men, friend drama, or work?

IRIS:

I can bring Nancy into the fold if it's about relationships!

I laughed. I loved Nancy, but sometimes her advice was biased towards sex. Actually, most of her advice was.

ME:

We leave for Morgan's wedding tomorrow. Jay and I are driving together since we both have to be there early for bridal party stuff. Morgan knows the truth, but her parents don't. I'm nervous about how to act. Especially since Jay seems so carefree about the whole thing.

My sisters knew about the fake engagement, just like Morgan did. So did Mom and Auntie. Everyone was a bit shocked at first, but mostly because of the speed at which we got engaged, not that we were together in the first place. In fact, everyone's response fell into one of three categories—"about time," "I knew that boy would wise up eventually," or "quick but not surprising."

I didn't understand how everyone could be so blasé about it. Yes, I liked Jay—a lot. Yes, we had history. But it wasn't normal to get proposed to on your third date and then keep the fake engagement story going. Right?

> HAZEL:
>
> Just act like you would if you were dating.
>
> IRIS:
>
> You were already dating before the proposal, so just keep that going and don't worry about the engagement part.
>
> ANNA:
>
> If people ask you about it, just keep your answers simple.
>
> HAZEL:
>
> Or make Jay answer. He's the one who got you into this.
>
> GALE:
>
> I wish I could offer you advice, but I've never been in a relationship, let alone been fake proposed to, so I'm not much help. But I love you and am sending far away good luck!

I smiled. These women had my back no matter what happened, and even though I was only blood-related to one of them, I knew every single one of them would stand with me in any situation.

Talking with them had given me the little boost of

confidence I needed to handle this weekend. And I would need all the help I could get.

It was Friday morning, and Jay was going to be here in just a few hours to pick me up so we could head home to Stratus Cove, California for the wedding.

My chat with my sisters had helped, but only marginally, which would explain why my hands were twitching like I'd had too much caffeine, despite not having a single cup of coffee yet.

I was all packed. Frizzle was taken care of and set for the next two days while we were away. But I was jittery. So, I decided to pull out some work stuff and try to finish up some of my burn scar reports.

In the last two weeks, I'd collected dozens of photos and videos from the fire scenes, but I couldn't shake the feeling that I was missing something. Technically, it wasn't my job to solve who had set the fires. My role was to determine flood potential, mudslide risks, and soil stability.

But Mother Nature was good at leaving clues if you knew how to read them. Clearly, I was blind, because I was missing whatever clues were out there.

We already knew the fires were intentional. No lightning, no down trees, no accident. Nope, this had full-blown intent.

The deaths may have been unintended, but the fires

weren't.

I was stuck, but if there was one person who could help me find the clue like it was a fingerprint in the crime, it was Gale.

My sister was a forensic meteorologist—not the forecasting kind, but the kind who testified in courtrooms after building evidence against the bad guys. Gale specialized in reconstructing weather events using satellite and radar data. People often thought radar was only used for rain and snow, but it could also show smoke. Those smoke plumes would show up mere minutes after ignition, revealing prevailing wind direction and projected spread of the fires. She also used surface observation stations, which could record haze and even temperature spikes when the fires got close—until they melted the sensors.

Gale didn't just look at storms and fires...She dissected them. And I needed that expertise.

I pulled out my phone and shot her a few quick texts. I would have called, but she was an introvert to the max and preferred texting. She also wasn't a morning person, and since it was still before eight, I knew she may not respond right away.

ME:

I need help with these fires.

ME:

Four of them. All arson, but I feel like I'm<br>missing something.

GALE:

Since when do you help solve cases?

ME:

I don't, but for some odd reason I'm
drawn to these, and I can't let it go.

GALE:

Send me whatever data you have. I'll
look at it after I've had my coffee.

I smiled—she was in!

I emailed her everything I had—photos, videos, and the fire line charts, as well as data I wasn't really required to look at but felt compelled to. Radar sweeps showing the wind direction and shift of the fires, as well as the GOES satellite thermal bands, all time-stamped and color-coded with the ignition points marked.

I hit send and hoped that she could see something I had missed so we could catch this guy and prevent any more fires and fatalities.

Then I waited for Jay to pick me up and hoped there wasn't a disaster of a different kind this weekend at the wedding.

# 17

## Jay

The highway spread out for miles in front of us. The desert landscape gave way to the pine-covered hills as we rolled toward home. The drive from Reno to Stratus Cove was exactly six hours, forty-one minutes, and seventeen seconds of me trying not to stare at Cora's legs while she talked.

She had on a cute sundress that ended mid-thigh, giving me the perfect view of those long, gorgeous legs the whole drive.

Her window was cracked open, her hair whipping around like she was in a low-budget car commercial. I kept my eyes on the road—well, mostly—but every time I glanced over, she was either talking animatedly about her family or laughing at something.

We talked about her family because I'd always been

terrible with names, and she had so many members of her family that it was easy to forget who was who.

"Gale is the oldest, and she still lives at home with Mom and Auntie on the farm."

"Oh. Is she gonna take over the farm someday?" I asked.

"I don't know," she replied. "She's a forensic meteorologist but works remotely, so she has a full-time job. I think she just likes the comfort of living in a familiar place and doesn't do well around new people."

That made sense. I remember her oldest sister because even though she was a year older than me age-wise, she had been held back, so she was in my grade in high school.

"You're next in age, but is Iris after you or Anna? I get them confused."

"Yes, I'm next in line, followed by Iris, whom you saw at the event with us," she replied. "Then Anna is next, and she lives in Atlanta with her husband. She's a TV anchor, and her husband is a private investigator."

"Oh, that's cool. I think I remember Morgan telling me Anna was the only freshman to work on the school newspaper, so that makes sense she would end up being a journalist."

I always found it fascinating to see where people ended up after high school. Maybe because my life hadn't turned out to be anything like I had thought it would be, I was always interested to see how other people's lives worked out.

"Finally, there's Hazel, who is currently a marine biologist at an aquarium and lives in a coastal town not far from Mom and Auntie."

Her face lit up when she talked about her family. I loved seeing her this happy.

We pulled into a gas station just outside of Redding, the kind with a flickering neon sign that seemed to be working on a part-time basis.

Cora went inside to use the restroom while I filled the tank. I drummed my fingers on the pump, counting down the seconds. When she returned, she was quiet, thoughtful in a way that made me pay attention.

We had just gotten back on the highway when, out of nowhere, she said, "Do you ever feel like everyone else has their life together except for you? I think about your sister, and all of my sisters, and how they all just seem to have everything together in their lives, and I don't. They're all either married or about to be married, except for Gale and Hazel, but neither of them *wants* to get married, so they don't count. They all have their jobs and feel content."

I tried to interrupt, but she kept right on talking without missing a beat.

"Don't get me wrong... I have a great job—my dream job—but something just feels like it's missing. I just wonder sometimes if it's me. If I'm the problem, like I'm doing something wrong."

I didn't answer right away because I didn't know what to say. I understood, though. More than most people, I knew what that felt like, especially when everyone around you seemed to have their shit together and your own life didn't turn out like you'd thought it would.

I may not have known exactly what to say, but I knew I needed to say something, and I needed to have her full attention when I did.

I turned the wheel and pulled off the road and into the parking lot of an abandoned warehouse. Windows were boarded. Weeds were growing through the pavement.

I killed the engine, and then I turned to her. "Cora," I said, my voice calm but measured. "I'm not sure where this came from, but I get it. I know what that feels like more than you can even know. I watched friends graduate from college at the same time my baseball career had completely fallen apart. I questioned every decision I had made up to that point as I watched other people turn more successful and my life going the opposite direction."

I saw sympathy form across her face, and I knew I needed to steer this conversation in a new direction. "But you can't compare yourself to other people. You're smart. You're funny. You're beautiful even when you're covered in cat hair. You're the kind of person who remembers everyone's name even when they don't deserve it. And you're the only one who ever saw me—the real me—in high school. Everyone else just noticed the guy who might end up becoming a professional baseball player, but you saw me for something else."

She blinked. "That was...weirdly sweet."

"I'm not above weirdly sweet, especially when you're

sitting two feet away from me looking as beautiful as you do."

I didn't wait for her to argue. I leaned over to cup her face in my hands and kissed her.

She didn't pull away. She kissed me back hard and hungry, like she'd been waiting for this too. I slid my hands down her back, attempting to pull her closer, but she was stuck. Before it even registered, I heard her unbuckle her seat belt, and she shifted until she was half on my lap, her legs straddling mine, her fingers tangled in my shirt.

We were both breathing fast. Hearts pounding, clothes getting wrinkled, the world outside my truck completely forgotten.

She broke the kiss first, her wide eyes now dark as midnight.

"This might be a bad idea," she whispered.

"Maybe. But it could also end up being your favorite bad idea." I wasn't above persuasion to get what I wanted, and I wanted Cora. I wanted her so damn badly. "Sometimes bad decisions come with good intentions."

I kissed her again, sliding my hands to the thin straps of her dress and lowering them over her shoulders, feeling her soft, silky skin under my fingers. Goosebumps formed as I ran my fingers from her arms, up her shoulders to her back.

Feeling bold, I worked the back of her bra and swiftly unclasped it. I moved my other hand to her front, pulling her pink bra down and lifting to cup her breast in my hand.

She gasped, causing her mouth to separate from mine, but she stayed close. Her eyes met mine, and I watched the silent inner workings of her brain as she tried to figure out what to do next.

"Take what you need, Cora."

"I don't know what I need," she replied, her breath ragged.

"Yeah, you do," I whispered my encouragement. "You need me. Just like you always have."

She bit her lip, deep in thought, and it was sexy as hell watching her brain process whatever she was thinking. I rolled my hips upward, my throbbing hard cock stretching my jeans to their limit. As the rough fabric rubbed against her, she moaned.

I shifted my mouth to the side of her head and whispered into her ear. "You want me to take care of you, and I'm here to do that. Let me take care of you."

She pressed her hips down against my cock, and I had to reel in my control, or I'd come in my pants just from her movement.

I moved my hand between her legs and gently stroked my fingers over her soaked underwear. Moving them aside, I slid one finger inside her, causing her to make the most amazing sound of pleasure. She was drenched, and I planned to make her even more so. I added a second finger, and she was wrapped around me so tight that I couldn't wait to feel that hot, wet heat around my dick.

"I need more, Jay." Her voice was soft as she made her command. "I want you inside me, please."

"I am inside you," I teased.

"More," she whimpered as she ground down against my fingers.

"God, Cora, you were made for riding me," I said, staring up at the beauty of her. "You look so damn good taking what you need from me. Take it, sweetheart. Take what you need from me."

"Jay," she moaned, and then she came undone. Her pussy clenched tight around my fingers as she came. I watched as her face became even more beautiful as she unraveled before me.

I knew at that moment that I needed to play my cards right so I could convince her to keep this engagement going and marry her for real.

Two hours later, we entered the lobby of the grand hotel where the wedding would take place tomorrow. It felt like stepping into a Pacific Northwest retreat, but with the rustic feel of a Yosemite or Yellowstone National Park vibe—towering wood beams, a massive stone fireplace, and giant candelabras hanging overhead. I saw why my sister had picked this place to get married.

As we moved toward the reception desk, I saw my mom and sister standing off to the side with some other woman I didn't recognize.

"You know who that woman on the left is?" I asked Cora.

"Since you don't know her, I'm assuming she isn't related to you, so either she's the wedding planner or someone from the groom's side of the family."

"Jay! Cora! You made it," my mother practically shouted from across the room, even though we were now less than thirty feet from them.

She hugged us as my sister introduced the other woman. "Cora, Jay, this is Brianna, my wedding planner."

"So nice to meet you," Brianna greeted us, and we shook hands. "Why don't you guys check in to your rooms, freshen up, and we'll all meet in the central ballroom for the rehearsal and dinner at six o'clock."

"Yes, I'm sure you're both tired, and want to relax for a bit," my mom said.

"Do we have to tell them anything since you got the rooms for us?" I asked my sister, but she just looked at me weirdly.

"What do you mean?" Morgan asked.

"The room block," I reminded her.

"Oh, God," Cora whispered beside me.

I looked down at her and noticed she had her hand covering her mouth, trying not to laugh.

"You didn't book a room, did you?" my mom asked, though it was clearly a rhetorical question.

"Morgan said in her text she arranged a block of rooms for all the bridesmaids and groomsmen," I replied, proving my case.

"Yes, that means I told them to save you a room, but you still had to book it and pay for it, dumbass," Morgan shot back.

"Don't call your brother a dumbass," my mom chided her.

"But he's being a dumbass," she defended.

I tried to argue with her, but Cora pulled my arm. "I'll go help him get a room. Don't worry about it."

"There are no more rooms left," Brianna chimed in.

*What did she just say?*

"She's right," my mom added. "They're sold out. We just tried to get your cousin Raquel a second room so her kids had more room to run around in, and they're fully booked."

*Crap. Now what do I do?*

"Maybe you could share Cora's room?" my mom suggested.

Okay, maybe this wasn't the worst thing to happen.

"You are *engaged,* after all," Morgan teased, and I knew Cora must have told her it was a ruse, based on the look on her face.

"Perfect. Problem solved." My mother clapped her hands together in excitement and then turned to Cora. "By the way, welcome to the family officially, dear. I couldn't be happier. He's definitely marrying up."

"Wow... I'm standing right here," I said to my mother in mock offense.

"Well, she's telling the truth," my father said as he walked up beside Cora.

He gave her a hug and welcomed her to the family, same as my mother had, and then turned to me.

"About damn time you came home," my father said, and the weight of what he said settled in my chest.

Cora's hand linked with mine, and I looked down at her, seeing the small smile on her face as she looked at me.

I knew she was giving me that because she knew I needed it to deal with my family, especially my dad.

Damn, this woman was something.

We made our way to the check-in desk, grabbed our keys, and took the elevator up to our room.

Her hand trembled slightly as she lifted the keycard to unlock the door. Personally, I was thrilled that we would be sharing a room, but I didn't want to make her uncomfortable by doing it.

We had a room with two queen beds, a small desk area with a tiny couch, and a bathroom. It wasn't a tiny room, but it also wasn't a suite.

"Two beds for just you?" I lifted my brow in question, a little bummed there wasn't just one big king bed for us to share.

"I originally booked the two queen beds because Morgan had said she might stay with me the night before the wedding. She decided to go with a different plan, but I never bothered to change my room." She shrugged.

"Which bed do you want?" she asked me as she set her bags just inside the room.

"What about the same one you're sleeping in? Is that an option?"

She rolled her eyes at me but said nothing.

"Cora, I thoroughly enjoyed our time on the car ride here...especially the part where we stopped and parked." I paused as I noticed her cheeks getting pinker by the moment as she likely recalled the same memory. "As much as I am dying to do that again, we move at your pace. If you want your own bed, you pick whichever one you want. But I'm hoping by the time this weekend is over, your question will be a moot point."

She stared up at me silently, but I didn't miss the heat in her eyes.

"I'm gonna hop in the shower." I leaned down and gave her a quick peck on the cheek and whispered in her ear. "You're welcome to join me."

I heard her deep inhale before I pulled back and winked at her. I grabbed my bag and took it into the bathroom with me.

I'd told her the truth. I wasn't going to pressure her into anything, but I was also going to take any and every opportunity to tell her how much I wanted her and found her undeniably sexy.

I was also going to take every opportunity to show off my own undeniably sexy body. That included walking out of the bathroom ten minutes later in only a towel wrapped around my waist.

At first, she didn't notice me, but then she grabbed her

own toiletry kit, and her gaze settled on me as she began walking to the bathroom.

"You have...hair on your chest." It was more of a statement rather than a question, so I stayed quiet as she stood there gawking at my shirtless body. I had never been happier to be fit and toned, based on the way she was staring at me.

"Most men do," I replied with a cheeky grin.

"Well...yeah...but...don't a lot of them shave it or something?" she asked, stuttering and clearly nervous.

"Some do."

I usually did, but I'd gotten lazy this week since I had so much going on. Now I was glad I hadn't shaved it off since it was clearly keeping her interest.

I took two steps closer to her before dropping my voice low. "If you want, you can check out my other hairy spots, like my arms, legs... and just below my belly button there's this trail of hair that leads—"

"Wait!" she all but shouted, backing up and shaking her head. "I'm...I umm...I believe you. Just... Can you put a shirt on or something?"

She waved her hand flippantly at my chest, and her face was bright red.

"As my *fiancée,* this shouldn't bother you." I gave her my best sinful grin and continued my forward movement toward her.

She rolled her eyes, but the way she bit her lip betrayed her. "We're not really getting married."

"*Yet,*" I corrected, winking before turning toward the

bathroom. "I'll cover up and spare you the full view for now. But later? I have a feeling you'll be begging for an encore."

Her breath hitched, and she stayed planted like her feet had forgotten how to function. "I'm going to get ready," she managed to say, even though she hadn't moved an inch.

I decided to move for her and walked around her side, heading to the empty bed at the far side, clearly the one she had deemed mine.

I heard her rustle some clothes together, and just as she started moving to the bathroom, I called out, "Oh, and Cora?"

She paused at the doorway and glanced back at me. "Yeah?"

"A couple kisses here and there aren't going to cut it. Not for me." I let my gaze drag deliberately over her. "And I don't think they're enough for you either, judging by our fun time in the car today."

She swallowed, and her cheeks flared again.

"We never went to prom together," I added, softer but still teasing. "So, tomorrow night? You're mine. And after the wedding? No curfew and no chaperones. Just you and me together, as we were always meant to be."

# 18

## Cora

I hadn't slept well.

I'd tossed and turned all night, mostly because of what Jay had told me yesterday in our room.

Thankfully, I'd slept in Morgan's room last night with all the other bridesmaids as we did a very low-key bachelorette party. Morgan had just informed us last night that she was eight weeks pregnant. They were keeping it a secret from the general public for a little bit longer, so she hadn't wanted to have a big night of drinking or going crazy.

We'd all just chatted, played some silly games, and crashed in her room. Was it fun sleeping on the couch in her room? No. But it was safer than going back to my room with Jay there.

After what we'd done in his car yesterday, I knew it was dangerous to be in the same room as him.

I'd clearly proven I had no control left when it came to that man—and part of me didn't even care—which was so scary.

My nerves hadn't gotten much better as I went back to collect my clothes and things for the day before going back to get ready with the girls. Thankfully, I'd timed it right and the room was empty.

I'd heard Mr. Rainer tell Jay last night at dinner that the guys were all going for a quick round of golf in the morning and they needed to be downstairs at eight a.m. sharp to make their tee time.

I was still a ball of nerves as I headed back to Morgan's room after breakfast to get ready with her and the other bridesmaids.

It was a fun distraction, getting our hair and makeup done and just chatting away.

"So, tell me about you and my brother," Morgan said, her eyebrows wiggling up and down.

The groom's twin sister, Laura, had practically swooned when we started talking about Jay. "I think it's so cute that your best friend and brother are getting married."

"It's the best," Morgan told her and then turned to me. "Spill, girl. Any more dates since I interrupted the last one?"

I chuckled. "Our schedules lately haven't allowed for

much, but we talk every day. He's sweet and soft and fun to be around."

"Did you just call my brother soft?" Morgan said and then laughed. "Jay is about as soft as a cactus. That man is prickly about *everything*."

I laughed because I had definitely seen him that way with Morgan, especially growing up. But with me, he seemed…different.

The other women chimed in about their husbands or boyfriends and whether they were prickly or soft-natured, and we all had a great time.

A few hours later, we were all dressed and ready to head down for the ceremony.

I walked into the private room where the bridal party would be waiting until it was time to go out to the central courtyard at the hotel for the ceremony itself.

Brianna was there in full wedding planner mode, directing all the bridesmaids and groomsmen on where to be and handing us our bouquets. I was heading to my spot when I heard a low voice behind me.

"You look so serious, future wife."

I sighed and turned to face Jay.

"You look so fucking beautiful," he said with so much heat that I was surprised I didn't spontaneously combust. "I thought you were pretty back in high school, but damn, Cora, you've grown up to be one hell of a stunning woman."

I moved my own gaze up and down his body, admiring

how good he looked in his black tux. His crisp white shirt underneath clung to him in all the right places, and he had a fuchsia bowtie to match our bridesmaids' dresses. He looked absolutely delicious.

My mind floated back to seeing him in only a towel yesterday, and my mouth salivated at the potential of seeing it again tonight.

I know I'd teased him, but I really did want to see it again. I wanted to see all of him. I knew it was a risky move to sleep with him, but my body craved his.

*There were worse mistakes to be made, right?*

"I like where your mind is right now," he said, his eyes intensely fixated on mine, "but let's table those thoughts for now since we can't do anything about it just yet."

He took two small steps closer to me—close enough for me to feel his body heat without actually touching him. "After the wedding...all bets are off, sweetheart. I'm going to let you have your merry way with me."

"You're going to *let* me, eh?" I mocked.

"Yep," he said, his lips mere millimeters from mine. "And then I'm going to kiss every square inch of your tantalizing body."

A wild riot of sensations rippled from my head to my belly to the now very wet space between my thighs.

His hands moved to my hips, and they seared into my skin through my dress. It felt like I was being branded by his touch, and my core temperature shot up.

"Everyone, line up!" Brianna shouted.

He leaned down and gave me a quick peck on the cheek before walking back over to the rest of the groomsmen.

I sighed deeply.

*Dear God.*

That man lit a fire in me like I had never felt before.

I fluffed my dress, brushed the loose hair on my forehead back, and tried to calm my thoughts and my heart rate.

The music began to play, and I made the mistake of looking up. The men were all going first, followed by the women. Jay was directly in front of me, and I watched in slow motion as he glanced over his shoulder, a wicked grin on his lips, and winked at me.

I was both equally excited and terrified about what was in store for me after the wedding was over. Excited because...well, it was Jay and I'd wanted this forever. Terrified because I had a feeling sex with Jay would complicate matters even more and make it that much more difficult if we ended things down the road.

He'd said he wanted to keep this going and had no intention of this not working, but you couldn't know these things so far in advance, could you?

I was a math girl, and statistically, roughly half of marriages failed, including my own parents'. That rate was even higher for quickie marriages.

*How was he so confident that this was meant to be forever?*

I wanted it to be true, but for me, the reality was that it didn't always work out that way.

I knew people made it work—my own sister Anna had a quickie Vegas marriage to her husband—but I still worried. I knew deep down, though, whether I was ready to admit it or not, I was worried because I was already half in love with this man, and if it didn't work out, I wasn't sure I would ever recover.

An hour later, after the ceremony and after nearly a million photos were taken, we were in the reception area eating our meal. I was seated at the far end of the long table with the other bridesmaids. Jay was at the other end of the table with the groomsmen. We may not have been seated together, but every time I looked in his direction, his eyes were on me.

Every. Single. Time.

The bride and groom finished their dance, and Morgan moved seamlessly into her father's arms while her new husband took his mother's hand, and the four of them shared the dance floor.

I watched them as something in my chest tightened. Last check, my own father was still in prison, this time for a different crime. Not that I'd want him standing beside me on my big day like this, but there was a quiet ache in knowing I'd never have that moment—the simple ceremonial spin across a dance floor with the man who was supposed to show up for you. The man who was supposed to put his children above himself.

I must have drifted deeper into that thought than I

realized because I didn't hear anyone approach. A hand appeared in front of me, palm up, followed by a familiar deep voice at my ear.

"May I have this dance, Cora?"

I wanted to hesitate. To play hard to get. Maybe give him a tease of a "Hmm, let me think about it" sort of line, but my body had other plans.

My hand acted of its own accord, stretching out to take his. I stood from my chair and followed him as he led us to the dance floor.

My heart was hammering like I'd just sprinted a mile in heels.

My high school self had dreamed of a moment like this, dancing with him in a sexy suit, me in a dress I felt beautiful in.

High school me would be doing cartwheels right now.

Current me was having a sudden overwhelming rush of adrenaline. The kind where your stomach fluttered and your brain short-circuited, and you were ninety percent sure you were about to pass out from sheer, stupid, glorious attraction and excitement.

We walked to the dance floor, which was filling with other people as the bride and groom finished dancing with their parents.

Jay pulled me close—not gently or politely—so I was flush up against him. His hand slid to my lower back like he'd been waiting for this exact moment too. I could feel the heat coming off his body and transferring into mine.

"I am the luckiest man in this building," he

murmured, voice low enough that only I could hear, "because I get to dance with the most beautiful woman."

My brain, which had only just begun to come back online, short-circuited again.

He didn't wait for me to answer. Instead, he leaned in closer, so close I could feel his breath against my ear. "I never got to take you to prom, so I plan to dance with you all night—both here on the dance floor and back in our room."

His eyes were dark, hungry, and locked on mine like he was already undressing me in his head.

Me? I was doing the same exact thing, but I wasn't going to let him see that.

"You seem awfully confident that this is going to happen between us tonight," I taunted him, even though we both knew it was inevitable. Mostly because I was pretty sure my lady parts would revolt if I denied them this golden opportunity.

His mischievous smile was making silent promises—promises I really wanted to come true. "Cora, a real man knows when the time is right to break down your walls —" he paused as he stared into my eyes "—and when to pin you up against one."

That was the moment my ovaries exploded.

At least, I was pretty sure that was what that feeling inside me was—like my reproductive system had just popped confetti.

I didn't say anything. I couldn't.

My mind was envisioning Jay pinning me up against a

wall and having his way with me, and there was nothing else my brain could seem to focus on.

He leaned in so close I felt his lips brush my ear when he growled, "You keep staring at me like that, and we're not going to make it to the end of this reception before I take you upstairs."

Okay, I needed to calm down. As much as I wanted Jay to take me upstairs, my duties as maid of honor needed to be upheld.

Thankfully, the song ended and gave me the excuse I needed.

"I'm going to get a drink," I said and then slowly walked to the bar area to catch my breath.

Jay was right, though. Some walls were meant to be broken. Others were meant to be broken while pinned against them.

Funny enough, I couldn't wait for Jay to do both.

After Morgan and her husband left for the night, I stayed to help Mrs. Rainer collect Morgan's gifts so she could put them in her car.

The whole time, I kept eyeing Jay from across the room. And every time I looked, his eyes were on me. Usually my butt, but sometimes my face or what I was lifting, but always on me.

I grabbed the final box Mrs. Rainer had given me to put all the gifts in as Jay walked over to me.

"You almost done? Or can I grab something?" he asked. "I'm here to speed this along."

His grin told me why he wanted to speed this along, and I wanted that too, so I pointed to the cards on the next table over and told him to gather them up.

I had just put the last gift in the box when I heard a voice I hadn't heard in years call out behind me.

"Jay, is that you?"

"Yes, it's me," Jay responded to her.

"It's me, Regina Wallis. We went to high school together."

Regina Wallis. She'd been the most popular girl in school and had made no secret of the fact that she had a crush on Jay.

"I'm vacationing with some girlfriends here and was peeking into the room to see what was going on, and I thought that was you tucked in the corner." Her voice was so saccharine sweet that it made me want to puke.

"Good to see you," he responded, and I could tell from the look on his face that he didn't remember her. That made me feel good inside.

"What are you up to?" she asked, taking a few steps closer. "Did you move back home?"

The look in her eyes was predatory, and I felt my body moving of its own free will toward him.

"No, I'm just here for Morgan's wedding. I live in Reno now," he responded, continuing to grab the cards.

I kept my eyes on her as I set the box on the table in

front of him and then put my hand on his arm. "Do you need help, babe?"

He glanced up at me and then my hand on his arm and gave a small, wry smile back to me. He knew what I was doing and found it funny.

"I'm sorry… Who are you?" Regina asked me, clearly not happy that I was interrupting her chance to flirt with Jay.

"I'm Cora O'Hara, Jay's fiancée," I told her, placing myself between her and Jay.

She looked at my hand with the ring on it, which I had strategically placed on top of my other hand resting over my stomach. She looked up at me and then over at Jay to have him confirm.

"Cora also went to high school with us, but she was in Morgan's class," Jay responded, putting his hands on my hips.

She stared at his hands, then back at him, and I noticed the change in her demeanor. "So, I guess this takes me out of the running?" she asked, as if my confirmation of this wasn't good enough.

I knew the question was meant for Jay, but I was ready to go upstairs, and this was only delaying it, so I decided to intervene. "You were never in the running. You're not exactly my type."

I heard Jay snort behind me and his hands at my hips squeezed a little, but I just kept strong.

"I meant…" Regina started to say, but I cut her off.

"I know what you meant, but he's mine and about to

marry me, so he's off-limits," I said politely while making my point very clear.

Her face went from sweet, to confused, to pissed off in just a few seconds. "Well, it was good to see you, Jay. Have a nice night."

I didn't miss the fact that she hadn't included me in that well-wishing, but she turned and walked away, which accomplished my goal, so I was happy.

I started to turn to grab the box when Jay's hands at my hips tightened. He allowed me to turn to face him but not leave.

"If I didn't know any better, I'd say you liked being engaged to me," he said with a sly grin.

While I was happy I'd done it, there was a part of me that thought maybe I had overstepped. However, not one to give in, I put on my bravest smile, held my head high, and looked him straight in the eye. "It has some perks."

"Oh yeah?" he asked with a large smirk, likely enjoying this. "Like what happened yesterday in the car?"

"No," I answered too quickly. "I meant people like Regina, who were not nice to Morgan or me in high school. She used to tease me that Morgan and I were destined to be single old cat ladies for the rest of our lives. It felt nice to be able to tell her we were together. Especially since she wanted you so badly back then and clearly still does."

"Yeah, well, I had an amazing make-out session in my kitchen at the end of my senior year, and it ruined me for all other women. And now I'm engaged to that same woman, so I clearly won."

My heart melted at his comment, but I didn't get to say anything in return because his mouth was on mine.

The kiss was great. And heated. And everything I had remembered from the car yesterday.

"Okay, you lovebirds, let's keep it G-rated for the kiddos," Jay's mom said cheerfully next to us, causing my head to jerk back as I tried to pull away.

He let me move away from him slightly, but not enough to lose contact. His left arm was still wrapped tight around my waist, holding me up against his side.

"Sorry, Mrs. Rainer," I said quietly.

"Cora, you're an adult." She leaned in and moved her fingers back and forth from me to Jay. "And about to be family. You can call me Mom or Donna."

"Okay, Mrs....I mean...sorry, I..." I couldn't get it together for some reason, and I blamed Jay.

"You two go on up for the night," she said, practically shooing us away. "Your dad and I have the rest of it."

I was going to protest and offer to help, but Jay beat me to it. "Thanks, Mom. Have a good night." He leaned in to kiss his mom on the cheek and then pulled me back through the ballroom and toward the elevator lobby.

Jogging was more like it.

"Jay, we could have stayed and helped," I laughed as I tried to protest while we waited for the elevator to arrive.

"Yes, but there's something else we need to do that's a bigger priority," he said. His face was so solemn and serious that I was a little worried we'd forgotten something.

"What?" I asked as we entered the elevator.

He pushed the button for our floor and then turned to me as the door closed. "This."

Then his lips were on mine, and they were ravenous as he pushed my body up against the wall. He licked my lips, causing me to moan slightly and open my mouth, giving him the entry he clearly wanted. He slipped his tongue inside as his hands moved down my sides and around to squeeze my butt.

Awareness and emotions rioted throughout my whole body. Heat and lust coursed through my veins as he kissed me like there was no tomorrow. My mind spun as I got lost in his kiss, his scent, and his touch all at once.

The elevator dinged as the door opened to our floor.

I was dizzy as he released my mouth and started to pull me down the hallway. I struggled to keep up with him as he practically dashed down the hallway to our room, my hand connected to his.

Half a second after we arrived at our room, he whipped out the keycard and opened the door. He pulled me in, flipping the deadbolt as soon as he closed the door, and then turned back to face me. His gaze intensified as it moved slowly from my legs to my chest to my face.

There was a level of uncomfortableness in me from the energy bouncing between us.

My voice sounded hoarse as I asked, "What now?"

His response was a coquettish smile as he took one slow step toward me.

I wasn't sure why, but for every step he took forward, I took one back, until the back of my legs finally hit the edge of the bed.

"What would you like to do, Cora? The ball's in your court, sweetheart."

I wanted him to kiss me again. Maybe have a repeat of what we'd done in the car.

Then I started to freak a little, not knowing what the right thing to do was in this situation. It wasn't every day an opportunity like this with your dream man presented itself.

His face softened, and I knew he was clearly picking up on my anxiety. "Cora, we can just go to sleep if you want to. I may be ready for more, but if you aren't, we don't have to take this any further."

"I want more!" I practically shouted and then slapped my hands over my mouth and up to cover my eyes as my cheeks likely turned bright red.

My outburst only made his smile grow bigger and sexier.

In fact, I think my reproductive organs may have just self-combusted from the weight of his stare. Regardless, the voltage between us skyrocketed, heat pooled between my legs, and my heart raced faster than a greyhound.

"I'm just gonna go...umm...brush my hands...and uh...wash my...teeth."

I nodded, though I wasn't sure if that was directed at him or me.

I went into the bathroom, washed my makeup off, brushed my teeth, and took the time to calm myself down.

I wanted this. I wanted to have Jay make love to me and take that next step, but I was nervous. This man had the ability to wreck me, and I hated that someone had that amount of power over me emotionally.

*You can do this.*

*You are strong. You are confident.*

I stood up straight and walked out of the bathroom, determined to get naked with Jay and have a great night.

He was still in the same spot where I'd left him. The only difference was that he had removed his tie and unbuttoned the top two buttons of his shirt.

He smiled at me as I walked toward him—as if he sensed my confidence had come back.

"Take your clothes off, Cora," he commanded in his deep, sultry voice.

"You think I'm just going to do everything you say?" I tried to hide my nerves and keep my voice strong, but it definitely hitched as the words came out.

"No, but I can tell you're nervous, so I figure maybe it will be easier if you do it rather than me. Plus, I had to try, since I've been dying to say those words for more than a decade."

My stomach spasmed on hearing that from him. I had envisioned something similar.

"How do I know if you'd be worth my time," I teased, my voice sounding stronger than my confidence. "If you'd even be good in bed?"

I knew I was pushing his buttons with that one, but I couldn't help myself. It was what I did when I was nervous.

He gave me the most wicked and hungry grin I'd ever seen. "I've never had any complaints."

"Not to your face, at least."

*God, why was it so easy to needle him*?

But instead of being offended, his smile just grew wider. "Unzip your dress for me, Cora."

I did it. Truthfully, I had dreamed of him saying those words to me for over a decade as well. I wasn't going to betray fate now that my wish was being granted.

Plus, when he talked in that deep, sexy voice, it was hard to do anything but obey.

I needed him, and I needed him now.

I unzipped the back of my dress, pulled the straps over my shoulders slowly, and let the dress fall down around my ankles, never breaking eye contact with him.

I stood there in only my black lace strapless bra and my black lace thong. The way he looked at me sent thrills through my entire body.

I'd known there was a chance this might happen tonight, so I'd packed my sexiest undergarments—that would also work with the formal dress—just in case. Judging by the primal look in his eyes, I'd made the right choice.

The intensity in his eyes was like nothing I had ever seen before, and I loved every second of it.

"Damn, Cora." The words came out rough as he spoke and took one step closer. "I have dreamed about this exact moment for so many years."

He placed the palm of his hand on the side of my face and ran his thumb softly across my lower lip, teasing me, seducing me.

"So have I," I shared back quietly and waited for one of my biggest dreams to come true.

# 19

## Jay

She was perfect.

She stood in front of me in the sexiest bra and underwear I had ever seen. It was almost a shame to take them off her.

Almost.

My cock was hard as granite as it strained against my pants. I feared for the seam that was likely to burst at any moment if I didn't take these off.

"Looks like you need to catch up." She smiled at me as she pointed at my clothes.

"I think you're right," I said quietly.

I started with my belt, needing to give my dick some room to breathe.

I unbuttoned and unzipped those pants as fast as my

fingers would let me and dropped them down to my ankles. I toed off my shoes while I worked to unbutton my shirt, Cora's eyes fixated on me the whole time.

She swallowed, and I watched as her chest rose and fell, her breathing intensifying as she watched me undress.

"You sure about this?" I asked, because if she wasn't, I would stop, but I was praying she would say yes.

She smiled brightly at me. "Absolutely."

Down to only my boxer briefs, I moved toward her, cupped the sides of her head, and kissed her.

"Starting tonight, you are all mine," I told her, needing her to know this wasn't just going to be a one and done.

She stared up at me, and I saw the twinkle in her eye. "Is that your idea of encouragement or supposed to be a threat?"

I kissed her again, partly to shut her up and partly because she was irresistible and I couldn't help it.

I lowered her onto the bed and stared at her beneath me. Her cheeks were flushed, her eyes filled with molten heat. I needed a moment to just relish this.

"God, Cora, I've had this fantasy so many times," I told her, brushing her hair softly from her face.

"Really? What umm...what happens in this one fantasy of yours?" she asked, licking her lips.

"It wasn't one, Cora. It was *many* fantasies."

"Show me," she said breathlessly. "Show me what happens in your fantasies, and I'll tell you if it matched mine."

I growled in response. Her wanting me to live out my fantasy, but also knowing she had one, too? That did me in.

I slid my hands down her sides and around to her back. She lifted slightly as I moved to unhook her bra. The instant it was undone, I whipped that sucker off and threw it behind me somewhere else in the room.

I dragged my mouth down her neck and collarbone to her glorious chest, where I flicked my tongue over her pert nipples.

She moved her hands to my head and sifted her fingers through my hair, occasionally tugging as I worked my mouth over her body.

My hand moved south between her legs, and I stroked my fingers over the soaked fabric of her thong. Her body jerked as my fingers brushed over her most sensitive spots.

"Jay." Her needy whimper told me she needed more.

I dipped my finger between her legs, pushing her panties to the side and sliding through her wet core. Knowing she was already this wet for me, a quiet surge of confidence and triumph rolled through me. She wanted me just as badly as I wanted her. That realization went straight to my ego, in the best way possible.

I pulled back and moved to slide her thong off, doing it slowly and taking my time so I could catalog and remember this moment.

"I can't wait to taste you. To feel you come on my

tongue," I mumbled as I peppered her stomach with kisses and moved my way south.

She was on her back on the bed, staring at me as I opened her thighs and ran my hands from her knees to the promised land.

Once there, I didn't waste time. I flicked my tongue, swiping over her slick pussy, enjoying all the needy sounds she was making as I worked her over.

"Oooh, that feels so good," she moaned, her pelvis bucking up as she tried to get closer to me.

I loved that I was making her feel good. I'd wanted every woman I'd ever been with to feel good, but with Cora, there was this territorial need to be the only one to do that for her—and do it well.

My fingers and mouth worked in tandem to bring her to the edge, but I wanted her to come while I was inside her. So, I paused in my efforts and stood back up.

"What.... Wait... Why did you stop?" she whined beneath me.

"Because I need to be inside you."

I turned to grab the condoms I had put in the night-stand drawer earlier. I slid my boxers off as I ripped the condom package with my teeth.

I moved back over her and lined myself up at her entrance, staring down at her.

"This is it, Cora. There's no going back. Are you sure?"

She nodded, licking her lips. "Yeah. I want this. I want you."

"You're mine," I told her as I sank inside her wet pussy

and buried myself deep. "I think you've always been mine."

Her sharp inhale, followed by a low moan, nearly did me in, and I had only been inside her for half a second.

She was so tightly wrapped around me. So wet and warm.

"God, you feel better than I ever imagined," I told her as I moved slowly back and forth, enjoying every stroke.

"Jay." Her voice was barely above a whisper as she closed her eyes and tilted her head back.

Seeking an opportunity, I leaned forward and kissed her neck, sucking on the pulse point until she moaned even louder.

She squirmed beneath me as I explored her with my hands and mouth.

She wrapped her legs around my waist, allowing me to dive even deeper inside her.

I felt that familiar prickle move down my lower back, letting me know my orgasm was close.

I stilled, trying to get my shit together. I was not about to let our first time be bad for her. I closed my eyes and tried to breathe past the pressure that was already starting to build.

Control. I needed control.

I fused my mouth with hers, tongues swirling as I moved inside her.

I moved my finger to her clit and rubbed in slow, intense circles, watching her reactions for cues as to what she liked.

"I'm so close, Jay. I need…please…just…"

Once again, I took her mouth as I moved inside her, taking her in long, deep thrusts.

There was no finesse now, just frantic desire.

The harder I fucked her, the more she seemed to like it, so I gave up any idea of grace and poise.

Her back arched as she breathlessly called out my name. Then she shattered to pieces right in front of me, her pussy pulsing and squeezing like a blood pressure band around my dick.

Her cries of pleasure were throaty, raw, and oh so real.

I had wanted to keep going—give her multiple orgasms before I came—but that wasn't going to be an option.

I rode out her orgasm with her, making sure she was good, and then I let go and tumbled over the edge with her.

"Fuck, Cora." I released everything I had as I let the pleasure wash over me.

It felt like forever for our breathing to regulate as our sweaty bodies lay there together, still tangled.

"I think I need a shower, but I can't move my legs," she spoke softly, her words putting a small smile on my face.

I turned to face her, needing to tell her something before she left this space.

"You understand this isn't fake anymore, right?" I

paused, needing her to understand. "You're mine and I'm yours."

"Jay..."

I cut her off so I could explain myself first. "What's building between us, Cora? This is real to me in every way. All of it."

"Even the engagement part?" she asked nervously.

I wanted to tell her that, yes, that was real for me too, but I sensed she wasn't on the same page with me there yet. Still, I wanted to give her something.

"I love you, Cora. It's a little scary how much I do, but I can't change who I am or how I feel, and I wouldn't want it any other way."

I'd expected shock, maybe disbelief, because we hadn't been dating that long. But what I saw in her eyes wasn't hesitation. It was reciprocation. She was right there with me. She stared back at me, and the emotions were so obviously written all over her face.

I could tell she felt the same way but was nervous to say it.

"You don't have to say it back," I told her, not wanting her to feel pressured. "Just know that I like having you wear my ring, so it lets all the other competition know you are taken."

She smiled and shook her head. "You're ridiculous."

"Ridiculously handsome. Ridiculously gifted. Ridiculously sexy. Why, thank you," I told her and then proceeded to kiss that smile off her face. "Go get your shower, woman. Next round, I need more time to explore."

The heat in her eyes returned, and I knew she was just as excited for a second round, but she hopped up and quickly made her way into the bathroom.

An hour later, I took her again. This time slower, softer. I made love to her as I stared into her eyes. I knew she was right there with me, feeling this was more than just sex. More than just a fake engagement.

Sex with Cora was everything I had always thought it would be.

I knew that after tonight, I would stop at nothing to keep Cora mine forever. I just needed her to get there with me so the engagement didn't end after I got the new job.

As much as I wanted the job, I wanted the woman nestled up next to me even more. That was both a joyful realization and a scary one. It left me feeling both content and also scared.

Because if Cora left, she would burn me so deeply, I knew there would only be scars left behind.

# 20

## Cora

It was a few days after the wedding, and I needed my sisters. I needed advice, and I couldn't go to Morgan because she would totally be biased. But I also didn't even know where to begin.

My sisters knew I had crushed on Jay when I was younger, that he was now back in my life and interested in me. How did I explain that we fell into the lie of being engaged, and that had now spiraled out of control and I didn't know what to do?

I didn't have the answer, but I needed them, so I decided to just bite the bullet and start the conversation.

ME:

I love how fresh my bathroom smells when I kill a spider with an entire bottle of Febreze.

There. That sounded funny but would get their attention, and hopefully I could find a subtle way to change the subject.

HAZEL:

Are you ok?

ME:

Yeah, the spider is dead, so it's all good.

HAZEL:

That's not what I meant. You never randomly text us with something like that.

ANNA:

What's wrong?

IRIS:

Emergency sister FaceTime call!

GALE:

Give me two minutes. I'm feeding Bob and Larry.

Something told me she would need a bit more than two minutes to feed the llamas, because they were a handful.

I took a deep breath, knowing this would be exactly what I needed, even if it made me nervous as hell.

Nearly ten minutes later, my phone rang in my hand, and I swiped to open the group call.

"I'm driving so you can't see my face, but I'm here," Anna said, causing me to look at the others on the call.

Gale was at home, Iris was at her office, and Hazel appeared to be at the grocery store.

I gave them the rundown of what had happened at the wedding—all of it.

"We've got you," Anna said, and my sisters all took turns dishing out advice, moral support, and offers to send me door delivery of pints of ice cream for my emotional wellbeing.

"Are you still coming here tonight?" Iris asked me.

"Yes, I'm packing up and getting ready to head to the airport soon," I replied.

Monsoon season was upon us, and the Las Vegas Weather Service office was short-staffed right now, so I'd been asked to come down and support and coordinate with their office for temporary duty.

I hated to leave, though, because there'd been yet another fire and another burn scar assessment to do, but Jade has assured me she would take care of it.

"I'll have Nancy join us for dinner, and we can get her opinion too," Iris added, and I chuckled nervously.

I loved Nancy, but I wasn't sure her advice was the kind I needed right now.

However, the advice my sisters had given was good, and I felt more confident than I had before. I knew I was falling for Jay—and hard. I thought I was just letting fear stand in the way of letting him fully in.

There were burn scars everywhere.

They dotted the landscape in every photo Jade sent me. She'd already gone out with the BAER crew to assess yet another suspected arson wildfire while I was in Las Vegas.

I was FaceTiming with her, the camera shaking as she walked around, making it hard for me to see some of the details she was narrating. Darren and his crew moved behind her, stepping carefully through the ash and scorched landscape. I even caught a glimpse of Jay in the background with his team.

"What's Darren so upset about?" I asked, hearing him bitching off to the side about something.

"This whole lot was lodgepole pines, which are being destroyed because of logging, so he's upset about losing them," Jade informed me. "It's one thing to lose a few of them due to the fire, because they will grow back, but this was a lot."

I mean, I got it. Trees and nature were his thing, but he was in for a world of hurt every time he covered a fire if he kept getting this upset about the trees.

"How's it going down there?" she asked me. "Any big storms causing problems?"

I glanced toward the southern horizon from my view

in the Weather Service parking lot, where towering cumulonimbus storm clouds were stacking higher by the minute.

I knew she was asking because most storms lost their punch before they made it from Las Vegas up to Reno, but this was a potent storm. If any system had the muscle to survive the journey north, it would be this one.

Monsoon season was here.

So was fire season.

Most years we just hoped they both didn't hit at the exact same time.

Unfortunately, today looked like it was going to be one of those times.

Wildfires didn't just burn vegetation—they altered the soil chemistry. Extreme heat could create hydrophobic layers, causing the ground to actually repel water instead of absorbing it. So, when you had heavy rain on a fresh burn scar, the water just rushed over top. A flash flood after a fire didn't *undo* damage—it multiplied it.

"Not good," I told her. "You're going to need to keep an eye on the radar."

"Will do," she said, knowing that a post-fire flood could undo everything the BAER team and fire investigators were trying to stabilize for the investigation.

Three hours later, my shift was finally over. Since Iris worked the same shift, we left at the same time and decided to pick up some dinner on the way back to her apartment complex.

I usually stayed with my sister when I visited, but now

that Hector was there with her, as their new house wasn't finished being built, I didn't want to hear them screwing like rabbits all night. So, I'd opted to stay with Nancy in her spare bedroom next door.

Once we arrived, Iris helped me carry in all the stuff—including my overnight bag—to Nancy's.

"Come in, ladies! I've got such a fun night planned for us," Nancy greeted as she swung open the door. "Did you get my hot wings?"

Nancy was pushing eighty years old, but she could put away some of the spiciest wings on any menu and not even flinch at the heat.

I aspired to be her when I grew up.

Nancy shuffled toward the kitchen, plating food and pouring drinks like she was hosting a dinner party for royalty instead of two tired sisters. I changed into something more comfortable while Iris ran back to her apartment to do the same and say hello to Hector before returning.

By the time we settled around the table, Nancy had already demolished three spicy wings and was diving into casual conversation.

She filled us in on her kids and grandkids, complete with dramatic commentary about which ones were making questionable life choices.

"Now, on to the steamy firefighter," Nancy said. "Give me *all* the details."

I choked slightly on my drink at her abrupt topic

change, though I should have known better, since she did that often.

She waved her sauce-covered fingers in the air. "I need a photo. Actually, several photos."

I pulled up the photos of Jay and me from the wedding and held up my phone as I swiped through them.

She fanned her face. "Oooh, he's a stallion. Usually I like 'em a little bigger like Hector, but this man is definitely fantasy worthy."

I nearly choked on my drink again. "Umm..." That was all I could say. Nancy had no filter, and sometimes there simply wasn't a response.

"News flash, dear...Being eighty doesn't make me blind," Nancy asserted. "I know what I like, and I like my men thick and juicy."

"Are you talking about a man or a steak?" Iris asked.

Nancy paused thoughtfully, licking hot sauce off her fingers.

"Both," she declared and then cackled, which sent Iris and me into laughter right along with her.

# 21

## Jay

A week later, we finally got the first big break in the case we'd had. Whoever had set the fires had slipped up.

It was another hot inferno of a day, despite it only being noon. Trent and I were out at the scene of one of the most recent fires with the BAER team and our supervisors to see what the suspect—or suspects—had left behind.

A few days ago, Thompson had informed us that the scope of the fires meant there might be more than one arsonist working together. Some of these fires had spread so quickly that it would have made it near impossible to safely leave the scene of the crime, unless another person was there to assist in some way.

It was pure speculation at this point, but it certainly made us think about a few other scenarios.

Our new evidence—tire tracks—had been the key to linking a lot of the fires together. Tire tracks from four of the fires had matched perfectly. While we had suspected these were all done by the same person, now we had proof.

The tracks cut across the soil in two clean and deliberate lines. They were deep and seemed almost...confident. Like whoever had driven here hadn't been worried about getting stuck—or caught.

Tracks from a vehicle—or even shoe prints—didn't always survive a fire intact, but we'd been lucky with several of these fires that the soil had been very compacted, so the impressions remained even after the vegetation nearby had burned away.

Based on the evidence we had, these tracks were likely left by a large truck, and a heavy one, either because it was large or because it was hauling a bunch of equipment.

The spacing between the tires was wide—wider than most midsize pickups. It leaned more toward a utility truck or a government vehicle.

I found myself scrolling through the trucks I knew. Not because I thought I knew the criminal, but to try to think of a good comparison.

"I don't know why these people think this is such a smoking gun," Trent mumbled to me as we walked back to our vehicles after listening to one of the fire inspectors detail the tracks. "Do you know how many people own trucks around here? Hell, half our station drives trucks."

I knew what he was talking about, but police used tire tracks all the time for their investigations, and it usually helped, so I wasn't as pessimistic as he was.

"Yes, they do, but it's not just the type of vehicle that matters, Tannin," Thompson said as he came up beside us, his tone sharp.

I knew it was likely directed at Trent and not me, as I'd heard through the grapevine that Thompson wasn't happy with what he'd said to Nicole. Trent had been given a five-day suspension—without pay—for his comments, but some people felt even that punishment had been soft. Thompson included.

"In this case," Thompson continued, "the direction of the tracks is unusual. The vehicle also didn't park far away. In fact, it pulled right up to the origin site, meaning they knew exactly where they wanted to start the fire every time and weren't worried about having enough time to get out."

I'd wondered about that, too. It was cocky to be that way, thinking you could outrun a wildfire that close. But oftentimes, cockiness led you to making stupid decisions out of either pride or sheer stupidity. Our arsonist likely fit the mold for both of those.

"Anything else you two pick up on?" Thompson asked.

I didn't know if it meant anything, but I figured at this point, anything could be mentioned.

"The tracks angled in from a service road," I told him. "A service road that most people likely don't know exists."

"Because it isn't on most maps, which means our arsonist is familiar with this area," Thompson confirmed. "Good work, Rainer."

I nodded at his compliment, feeling good about how I was fitting into this new potential role.

"That should be it for today," Thompson said. "There's a chance of thunderstorms, and I see some storm clouds off in the distance. I don't want to get stuck up here once it starts raining. Plus, we all need to get going for the fire-fighters' shindig, anyway. Let's pack up."

I looked back once more at the twin grooves pressed deeply into the earth. Whoever had done this hadn't panicked. Hadn't raced out of here. They'd taken their time. And that was what unsettled me the most.

"Hey, man, what happened to your car?" Blake yelled as I walked back into the station.

Thompson had just dropped us off, and I was going to grab something out of my locker quickly before heading home.

"What do you mean?" I asked, thoroughly confused.

"You've got a fuck-load of scratches all over the side of your car," Blake said, and my eyebrows shot straight up. "Looks like you got into a fight with a grocery cart and lost. Badly."

"No, man. I had no idea." I shook my head, wondering how I could have missed those. I grabbed my bag and walked quickly to the parking lot to see what he was talking about.

Sure enough, there were long scratches all along the passenger side of my truck. Three of them, in a perfectly straight line. If I'd driven too close to something and scraped it up, I would have known.

Shit. That wasn't going to be cheap to fix. I sighed, realizing there was nothing I could do about it at this point, and I needed to get home to get ready for tonight.

Despite the discovery of the damage to my truck, my entire drive home was actually spent thinking about the new evidence in the arson case. Would it be enough to catch this person? Would we catch them before another fire was started?

I sure hoped so. It wasn't just about the people who were killed, but also the damage that was being done and the resources these fires were eating up.

It was tough to shut my mind off when it came to cases like this. It was why I wanted this job so badly. It combined my love for firefighting, helping people, and also solving a mystery.

Once I was home, though, I tried to clear my mind. The ball was tonight, and I wanted Cora to be front and center for my attention for the entire evening and to not have to worry about work. I knew some work-related conversations would be inevitable since this was a work event, but most of us tried to avoid the heavy-hitting topics.

But this was going to be our big test. While some of my coworkers had already met Cora, the vast majority would be meeting my fiancée for the first time at the ball. I knew Cora was nervous because she didn't want anything to go wrong that could affect my job or my chances of getting my new role.

For me, though, tonight would be easy. There would be no faking on my end. I knew from the moment I saw her at that event in Vegas several weeks ago that I wanted to ask her out and get that second chance I had been dying for.

I may not have intended to propose to her the way I did, and part of me regretted not making it more special, but I didn't regret asking her. I knew with every fiber of my being that I wanted her to be my wife—to make a life with her.

In the two weeks since the wedding, Cora had traveled to Vegas, and we had both been busy with our jobs, but we'd made a little time every day to at least talk with each other.

Even if it was only for fifteen minutes in the morning, I would swing by her apartment to say hi and make out with her for a few minutes before she left for work. Just being able to see her face and hear her voice put a smile on my face.

I wanted this inspector job because it was what I

wanted to do with my life, but it would also give me a bit more normal hours. More time to spend with Cora was a huge appeal.

I realized I had showered and changed in record time, which meant I had two choices. I could sit on my couch at my apartment until it was time to leave, or I could go over to Cora's and sit on her couch while she got ready. Both options involved a couch and waiting, but the latter included Cora.

It was a no-brainer.

As I grabbed my tie, I looked around my room, realizing how empty this place was. For months now, it had been a place to sleep and eat, and I'd obviously treated it as such, having barely furnished it.

We had both just entered our thirties, and while I couldn't answer for her, I knew I was ready to settle down. I wanted someone to come home to after work, someone to share my day with, plan vacations with, and I wanted that someone to be Cora.

Now I just needed to show her tonight that this engagement didn't have to be just for show.

I grabbed my suit jacket and put it on a hanger to leave in my car—it was way too damn hot outside to wear it unless I absolutely had to. Then I put on my shoes before making my way out the door.

I smiled the whole way to my car, thinking about having Cora on my arm and spending the time with her.

I would prefer it if it were alone time, especially after

all the fun alone time we'd had at my sister's wedding and since then.

However, I was finding I was addicted to spending any time with Cora, no matter what it included.

# 22

**"'Controlled burn' is when I finally speak my mind."**
—*It's science*

## Cora

The knock on my door startled me.

It was the weekend after I returned from Vegas, and I was in my bathroom getting ready for the Firefighters' Ball. Jay wasn't supposed to be here for another thirty minutes, but I also wasn't expecting anyone else.

*Meow.*

"Who do you think it is, Frizzle?" I asked my cat, even though she ignored me and sauntered away, likely to hide somewhere.

I walked out to my apartment door in just my bathrobe. It was pink with white polka dots and came down to mid-thigh. It was also super cute, which I was thankful for in that moment since my peephole showed Jay on the other side of my door.

Worried that I had gotten the time wrong, I swung the door open quickly. "Are you early, or am I late?"

He chose not to answer right away but rather pushed his way in and closed the door for me.

"I was ready and figured I could just sit on my couch by myself until it was time to leave, or I could come over and sit on your couch until it was time to leave," he said, smiling. "The latter option included a pretty girl."

I shook my head at his ridiculousness but threw my hand out toward my couch as permission to have a seat. "I have to finish getting ready, but you're welcome to hang out on my couch."

I turned to head back to my bathroom, but he grabbed my hand and pulled me into him for a kiss.

It was a quick kiss, but no less wonderful than all the others.

With his mouth still pressed against mine, he spoke softly. "Definitely better than my couch."

I smiled but pulled back, trying to take a very serious stance. "Let me go so I can get ready."

"Do you need help getting dressed? I volunteer as tribute to help you with that daunting task."

I chuckled and shook my head some more. "I am perfectly capable of getting dressed."

"I know, but it would probably be more fun if I helped you."

His grin told me there would likely be help in getting this robe *off*, not necessarily in putting other clothes *on*.

I pointed my finger at his face and gave him my best

stern look. "Go sit on the couch. I'll be ready in fifteen minutes."

"Party pooper." His cunning smile told me I had won...for now.

Ten minutes later, I was standing next to my dresser, where I had set out my jewelry and sparkly hair clip that I was about to add now that my hair was all finished.

From the corner of my eye, I saw Jay walk to my doorway and lean against the frame, arms crossed with a wickedly erotic smile on his face.

God, that smile should be illegal.

As I took in his whole look, I felt that familiar flutter of excitement buzz through me.

It took me a moment to realize he had changed clothes—or rather, taken some off. He had been wearing a dress shirt when he showed up. If memory served me correctly, he had been wearing black pants and a white dress shirt with the sleeves rolled up to his elbows, and a red tie to match my dress. Now, though, he was shirtless and only in his pants.

"What happened to your shirt?" I asked, finding it hard to focus on anything but his bare chest.

"I came in to ask if you had a steamer or iron I could borrow, but I think I'd rather help you get dressed first."

"My iron is in the hall closet," I told him, trying to focus on my task, but he looked so handsome that it was hard to concentrate.

"Stop being so attractive—it's rude," I told him.

"You make it really hard to behave when you look this good," he said, carnal need filling his eyes.

I couldn't help but get turned on. I didn't know if I should climb him like a tree or take one of his branches and slap him with it.

"You're distracting me," I told him, turning back to the mirror to finish putting my hair clip in.

"But in a good way, right?" He walked up behind me, wrapped his arms around my waist, and brought his mouth down on my neck as he placed featherlight kisses the whole way down to my collarbone.

He worked to untie my robe and the sides parted.

He growled into my shoulder as he moved his hands up and down my sides, exploring my skin as though it were the first time he'd ever seen it. "God, you make me feral sometimes, Cora."

"Jay, I need to finish getting ready," I protested, but even I could hear how weak it sounded.

He continued to kiss along my neck, moving up to my ear before speaking in his low, smooth voice. "I can think of something better to do."

"Like what?" I asked, my voice hitching as he kissed the spot behind my ear.

"You," he growled as he moved to slide my robe over my shoulders.

He turned me and we started walking backwards toward my bed. I knew we shouldn't be doing this—we didn't have time—but I couldn't seem to stop my body. He worked to free my breasts from my shelf bra as the back of my thighs hit my bed.

He swiped his thumb over my nipple, causing it to harden like a rock, and I mewled. I literally mewled, like my cat. I didn't even know I could make that noise. "Jay…"

"You have no idea how many times I imagined you saying my name like that." His voice echoed in my brain as he latched onto my nipple with his mouth and pulled hard, rendering all of my brain synapses useless.

My orgasm went from zero to sixty in an instant. It was building quickly, but I knew I needed more.

I fell back onto the bed, and he came with me as he feasted on my breasts as if they were a starving man's meal.

He grabbed my thighs with his warm hands and spread them open wider as he ran his hands up to my core. He brushed across my bundle of nerves and I felt my arousal coat my inner thighs.

"Jay," I moaned even louder as I squirmed underneath him. "I need you."

He leaned back and started to unbuckle his belt and pants. "We're on a time crunch, but I promise to take my time later."

I honestly didn't care about later. I cared only about right now, and I needed him.

The minute it was free, I leaned up, grabbed his rock-hard cock, and guided it toward my core.

I ran my fingers up and down a few times, stroking

him, before lining him up and moving the tip in circles around my soaked entrance.

"Cora, I need to get—" he said, but I'd had enough.

I lifted my hips up to let him slide right in.

We both moaned at the same time before he took over.

I didn't know why, but it felt better, and he clearly felt the same, based on the noises he was making as he continued to thrust inside me.

"Your body is dangerously irresistible." He stared down at me, his breath coming fast. "I can't get enough of you."

He took my mouth as he continued to push in and out of me, giving my body what it craved.

I felt so full and stretched and wonderful all at the same time. He started driving in and out of me harder and faster.

This wasn't the lovemaking we'd had the night of the wedding or even earlier this week.

This was pure, animalistic sex at its best. I loved the primal look on his face as he plunged deep inside me.

Pressure was building, and I knew my orgasm was right there, just out of reach. "Jay, I'm so close."

He moved his fingers to stroke my clit, and it sent tingles through every vein in my body. That simple stimulation was the touch I needed to take me over the edge.

I cried out as waves of pleasure rippled through me.

I felt lightheaded but also like I was on cloud nine.

"Cora, I need to stop and get..." His voice was strained, but all I heard was stop, and I couldn't let him.

My orgasm seemed to continue on forever, and I didn't want it to end. "Don't stop," I pleaded.

I felt Jay continue to pump into me as my head floated in the air, surrounded by his intoxicating scent.

"Cora…" I loved the way my name broke in his throat.

I felt hot pulses inside me as my body finally came down from my high. I had never felt anything so good in my life.

"You undo me, Cora." He was panting as he tried to leverage himself above me so he didn't squish me. "Your body is like a pull I can't seem to resist."

"What if I don't want you to resist me?" I asked, still breathing heavily myself.

He smiled back at me as though he'd won the lottery.

"Don't shoot the messenger, but you might need to redo your hair," he said softly, running his fingers through it.

I rolled my eyes and gave him my best fake outrage. "Are you just the messenger, or are you also the underlying factor?"

"I'm just here to satisfy my woman." He grinned at me. "I can't help it if sex hair is a result of the divine pleasure I give you."

I laughed at his nonsense, but inside I was smiling as big as I could. "Let me up so I can go fix this sex hair you've given me."

He didn't move, though. He stared down at me as he stroked my cheek.

"We didn't use a condom," he said softly to me.

*Oh shit. That's why he must have been trying to stop.*

He didn't seem upset about this at all, but I could tell his eyes were scanning mine to see how I felt about it.

We had both already talked about being tested—him regularly with his job, and me doing it earlier this year because I wasn't convinced Darren hadn't cheated on me.

I'd also told him I was on birth control, but I wasn't a saint when it came to taking it on time.

I should be upset, or at the very least worried, but I found that I wasn't.

In fact, as I stood there in the bathroom and redid my hair and makeup, I found there was a little part of me that actually hoped we had made a baby.

The Firefighters' Ball was not what I'd expected. It was filled with glittering lights, loud music, a large supply of food, and tons of people—easily a few hundred.

Jay looked unfairly handsome in his black suit, made even worse every time he grinned at me throughout the evening.

He'd been introducing me as his fiancée to everyone we met, like I was a rare artifact that he had just unearthed.

"This is Cora, my fiancée. Yes, she's real. No, you can't have her," he joked with everyone, as I usually shook my head or laughed.

We had just finished meeting all of Jay's bosses—the

full BLTS sandwich, if you will—when Jay offered to go brave the long line at the bar to get us some drinks.

I started to make my way over to our table when he showed up.

Trent. The same man I had seen at the burn scar assessment a few weeks ago.

"Cora, fancy seeing you here." His demeanor was friendly, but it carried full creepy vibes.

"Hello." I kept it simple and tried forcing a polite smile.

He leaned in, not too close, but close enough to make me uncomfortable. "So, I have a question for you. Jay never brought you around to anything before, which is odd because usually everyone brings their spouse or partner over to work events."

He paused, clearly hoping I would take the bait.

"I'm sorry... Was there a question?" *Two can play at that game, jerk.*

"How long did you two date before you got engaged?" he asked, his voice still friendly, but the smile was slipping. "Just seems like perfect timing for him to get engaged once he realized I've jumped ahead for the fire inspector position."

My stomach dropped, not because he was wrong, but because he was right in the worst way. I was also a terrible liar and didn't want to be put in this situation.

I stuck with the simplest answer and the truth to get me through. "We've known each other since high school, Trent. I think our first kiss all those years ago and the feelings that went with it lingered, and we just couldn't shake it anymore and decided to date, and now we're engaged."

He looked at me as though he knew I was lying, but then his gaze moved from me to something behind me. He reached out to put his hand on my shoulder in what would appear to be a kind manner, but I knew it wasn't.

I didn't have to look behind me to know what it was he was looking at. I felt his presence before he ever said a word.

Jay didn't need to. His presence alone was a warning that I could sense, and I imagined Trent did too.

"I would suggest," Jay said, his voice low and dangerous, "that you remove your hand from my fiancée. Right. Now."

Trent didn't move or even blink.

The air between us crackled, not with electricity, but with a distinct threat.

"Touch her again," Jay said, quieter now, but somehow more terrifying, "and you're going to need a new hand."

Trent finally pulled back—slow and deliberate, like he was testing how far he could push.

"Oh, for the love of God, Trent, let someone else meet her."

The voice was loud, brash, and unmistakably female.

"I'm Nicole Spicer," she said, extending her hand to me and ignoring Trent like he was an annoying piece of lint. "I'm in charge of the EMS crew at the station. You must be the woman who finally tamed this son of a bitch."

She nodded toward Jay in a joking manner, and I smiled.

"That's one way to put it," I said, shaking her hand.

"This is my girlfriend, Amanda," she said, introducing the woman beside her.

Amanda looked at me with an intriguing smile, like she had just been handed a front-row ticket to the world's most dramatic soap opera and was living it.

"Well, his attitude has certainly changed now that you're around. He's far less of a stick in the mud than he was before, so thanks."

"I do my best to keep him in check," I said cheekily.

She laughed, loud and genuine, and I loved it. "Oh, I like her. Don't screw this up, Rainer."

Jay's hand tightened on my hip—not angry, just there. Grounding.

Nicole turned to Trent, still smiling, but her eyes were sharp. "Trent, Stetson is looking for you."

He turned to leave, but not before sending one final glare over to Jay and me.

Amanda, still grinning, leaned in toward me, nodding at Nicole. "I love this woman. She's like a human fire extinguisher. Puts out the drama *and* is good to have around."

I craned my neck to look back at Jay to see that he was finally relaxing and the tension was leaving his body.

I stage-whispered up to him and smiled. "You're lucky she's on your side."

He kissed my temple. "I'm lucky *you're* on my side."

Nicole clapped her hands. "Alright, lovebirds. Enough tension for one night. Let's all get a drink. And Cora, tell me everything. How did you meet up again after all these years? Did he try one of those cheesy firefighter lines to get you to agree to a date? How was your first date?"

I laughed, knowing she was going to get a kick out of what had happened on our first date—and second. I just didn't have to tell her they had only occurred a few weeks ago.

# 23

## Cora

The last few weeks since the Firefighters' Ball had been so stressful for both of us, but we'd also grown closer.

On the nights he didn't work, we had dinner together and he slept at my place. When he did work, we found a few moments here and there to chat on the phone or text each other about our days.

Jay had been doing two jobs at once many days—his regular firefighter job, as well as assisting on the fire investigations since there had been two additional wildfires. There had actually been a third one, but that one had been started in the exact spot lightning was detected on radar, so it was ruled natural instead of arson. But Jay and the rest of the team still treated it like the others in the beginning because they wanted to be sure.

I was also busy, because in addition to getting all my

work done for our annual water year analysis, I had been called out to several of the fires too, in order to do burn scar assessments. I'd done them before, so it wasn't hard, but never this many back-to-back.

The thing that kept me up at night about the fires was that they seemed random but also strategic at the same time. I couldn't put my finger on it exactly, but I knew in my gut that I was missing something.

I was back at the scene of the Coltster Fire, walking through the charred landscape and hoping something would stand out. Investigations weren't my thing, but I knew burn scars, and there was just something off about these fires compared to a lot of the other fires I had covered in years past.

Jay finally had gotten around to getting his truck into a body shop for the repairs to the scratches. Since I hadn't planned to leave the house today, he had borrowed my car to take to work and was going to pick me up to go out to dinner. But then my brain had started spinning, and I knew I needed to go back to the scene of the fire. I took an Uber to get here and texted Jay my location so he knew where to get me.

Jay was already on his way to get me but was still a good fifteen to twenty minutes away—plenty of time for a video call—so I decided to call Iris and Gale to pick their brains and get some advice.

I gave them the update on the fires and told them I felt like I was missing something. We talked it out, them asking questions and me answering as best I could.

"Those are really tall trees," Iris commented, looking at the landscape behind me. "Are those sequoias?"

"Doubt it. Usually those are found a bit farther west, but it's not unheard of for some of those to be on the eastern flanks of the Sierra Mountains," Gale chimed in with her botany expertise.

"Okay, well they look way taller than the other trees behind you," Iris noted.

"It's hard to tell because a lot of pines look the same, but I think those are lodgepole pines." Gale squinted as she tried to see behind me.

I didn't know as much about plants as Gale, but I had heard of both of those trees before. That's when my mind started racing. Why had I heard of those before?

I stared at the trees around me and then down at the charred ground. My gaze focused on the pinecones on what remained of the forest floor.

So many pines. So much of this landscape was scorched and dead, but the pinecones just sat there looking like they were sleeping and ready to start over once they "woke up."

"Pinecones," I muttered out loud.

That was when it hit me.

I remembered Jade's comment from a few weeks ago. "Sequoias are known for having their seeds released through their pinecones when temperatures get really hot."

*Like in a fire.*

"Gale, is it true that some trees only release their seeds

in a fire?” I asked, wondering if that fact I had heard weeks ago was really true.

“Yes, but only certain ones,” Gale replied, looking at me funny. “Some pinecones have resin inside them. That resin will only open up and release seeds if the temperatures get hot enough to melt the resin away.”

“Hot enough, like from a fire?” I asked as I started walking to the edge of the fire where some surviving trees still stood.

She stared at me for a moment, finally understanding where I was going with this. “Yes, especially in a fire.”

“The trees,” I whispered out loud. “What kind of trees, Gale?”

She didn’t reply right away, but I could hear her typing away on her computer.

“A specialized group of trees called serotinous cones are designed to only open and release their seeds during a fire or extreme temperatures,” Gale said, clearly reading it straight from her computer. “This includes jack pines, lodgepole pines, and some species of sequoias.”

I gasped. “That’s it.”

“What is?” Iris asked. “I feel like I’m missing something.”

“The trees!” I repeated. “Lodgepoles and sequoia pinecones only open in fires, and those were the trees all found at the fire origin points!”

“Do you know *for sure* that those trees were at the point of origin for every single one of the fires?” Gale asked, letting me know she had the same train of thought I had.

"No, but I remember Darren mentioning those names at all the fires because he was sad they were gone, but he said at least the cones would help make more trees in the future…" I trailed off at the end as the pieces started to come together.

"You need to call Jay. I'm with you on this. It looks like these areas were chosen because of the trees."

Gale's agreement gave me the confidence boost I needed. Our arsonist intentionally set the fires where they did because they had trees that would only reproduce if the pinecones reached a hot enough temperature to release the seeds. Sequoias were endangered and lodge-pole pines were cut down and used for timber, meaning we had been losing a lot of them over the years.

I needed to call Jay and tell him my theory. I also needed to call Jade to have her help me verify my theory.

"Be careful. That big rainstorm is on the way," Iris said.

I thanked them both and hung up as I made my way over to the tree line where the fire had supposedly started. It was summer, so we still had a couple of hours of daylight left, but it would also get dark quickly if that storm rolled in, so I needed to get my pictures quickly.

*Me: Meet me at the point of origin site when you get here. I think I found the motive for the fires!*

*Me: And I think Darren might be behind it!*

I rattled off a few more texts explaining my theory. My

phone buzzed as he tried to call me, but I hit ignore because I needed to call Jade first. She, too, had paid attention to the types of trees at each fire, so she would know if they were all serotinous or whatever that name of trees was that had the special heat-release cones.

I called her, and she answered on the second ring.

"Hey Jade," I said into the phone, breathing heavily as I walked quickly back to the fire site. "I think I know the motive behind the arson fires."

"What?" she asked into the phone.

"The fires were started because of the trees," I explained. "And I think Darren is behind it."

"Darren, your ex-boyfriend?" she asked. "The one who works for BAER?"

I knew she likely thought I was crazy, so I rushed through my explanation, hoping it would make sense. "The points of origin of all these fires were in forested areas that had certain kinds of trees. Lodgepole pines and giant sequoias, to be exact. Darren mentioned those at each of the events. I remember him being sad since one of them was highly endangered and the others were being chopped down a lot for timber. Remember?"

She didn't answer right away, and I thought I may have lost her. "Jade? You there?"

"It's not what you think," she replied, and I quickly realized her voice wasn't coming through on the phone, but rather right behind me.

I whipped around to see her and Darren standing there together.

Both of them were wearing fire gear. Not the protective kind we wore when we were doing an assessment, but what firefighters wore to protect themselves from a fire.

"We're losing so many sequoias every year, Cora. This is the best way to help them," Jade replied.

"But we've learned our lesson, and we're timing the fires right now so that nobody else gets killed," Darren replied. While his comment sounded sympathetic, there was no remorse whatsoever in his voice.

A rumble of thunder sounded in the distance, and I turned around to see that the sky had darkened significantly behind me.

All the final pieces came together. The gear they were wearing, the comment about learning their lesson, the storm.

"You're setting another fire," I whispered out loud.

"We don't want to kill anyone, but we need those pinecones to open," Darren said nonchalantly. "Tonight is perfect because it's going to rain. A natural way to get rid of the fire quickly, but after the pinecones have burned enough to release new seeds."

Just then, the gust front from ahead of the storm arrived, which caused the wind to increase and whip into a different direction. That's when I saw the smoke.

"You already set the fire?" I practically yelled.

"It's going to rain soon, Cora. This is a good thing!" Jade yelled.

"Shit," Darren said, staring at the flames, which were now fanning out in all directions thanks to the wind.

"It's okay. Look, you can see the rain right there in the distance." Jade pointed behind us.

"We need to leave—now," I told them.

"Cora!" I heard Jay calling my name in the distance.

"No!" Darren yelled. "Not until you agree that you won't say anything."

"Cora!" Jay's voice cut through the wind, getting closer and more frantic.

I spun around, heart hammering.

He was sprinting toward us, wide eyes locked on me, then darting to Darren and Jade, and then to the smoke now billowing to the side of us.

I knew he was trying to assess the situation based on the very little information I gave him in the texts, but I didn't have time to fill him in now. We needed to leave.

"We have to go," I told him, starting in his direction, but I watched Jay's eyes flare and panic set in quickly.

"Neither of you are going anywhere," Jade's voice cut in, full of anger and determination.

"Cora!" Jay shouted, pulling my arm toward him and then behind his body as he finally reached us.

My eyes darted in Jade's direction to see she now had a gun pointed loosely in our direction. Jay was using his body as a shield.

"I'm sorry," she said, seemingly truthful but serious, nonetheless. "I didn't want to have to shoot you, but this is for the greater good."

"What are you doing?" Darren shouted. "You said you brought that to help start the fire if we needed it."

"Yes, but it also serves another purpose," Jade replied. "If we get caught, our mission to help the forests will be lost."

She was seemingly calm throughout this, despite the fire raging behind them and the weapon in her hand.

"We've already killed innocent people with these fires. I'm not adding others," Darren sparred. "It'll just bring more attention to this and more authorities that we don't need."

"If they leave, they'll *tell* the authorities, which is why I have my gun!" Her voice became more high-pitched and frantic.

I was trying to think of how to get out, but there wasn't exactly anything I could hide behind within jumping distance. Plus, I wasn't leaving Jay at risk of being shot either.

"Darling, listen to me," Darren said, trying to calm her, but I stuck on one word in particular.

"Darling?" I asked incredulously, shaking my head in shock.

"You weren't good enough for him, but I was," Jade spat back. "Once you let him go, I swooped in."

*How long had they been together? Jesus, maybe he really was cheating on me!*

The wind whipped behind us as the fire grew.

"Guys, we all have to leave now," I told them. "Yes, the rain will put out the fire, but it will also flood this whole area, turning this burn scar into a mudslide. You *know* that, Jade."

I pleaded with her to understand, but it was Darren who sold her.

"The fire is spreading too fast for the rain to catch up. We have to go grab the equipment and get back to the truck now, or neither of us will be able to help future forests," he told her, grabbing her arm and yanking her in the direction of the smoke.

She growled, but he was stronger than her so he was able to pull her away from us.

Not wasting any time, Jay pulled me in the opposite direction and started sprinting to my car.

He yanked open the passenger door, and I slid in just as a large wind gust slammed into us, the wind howling like a warning.

Behind us, I could hear Darren screaming something.

Jay rounded the car and hopped in, quickly locking the doors. "I need to call this fire in really quick."

I turned to Jay and grabbed his arm, my voice trembling but sharp. "Wait until we get down the hill. Jay, when that rain hits, it's going to wash out the only road out of here. The whole burn scar area is going to turn into a riverbed. We *need* to go—now!"

He didn't argue. He didn't ask for proof. Just nodded once, sharp and decisively. He slammed the gearshift into drive and hit the gas.

Out the side window, I could see the fire growing. It wasn't just a few small flames and smoke—it was a living thing, fed by wind and dry fuel from the remaining trees and plants not scorched by the previous fire.

A few raindrops started to hit the windshield, but there weren't nearly enough to put out the fire—yet.

We came to the fork in the road, and I knew Jay would try to head for the main road.

"Turn left," I told him, leaving no room for argument.

"But…" he tried to say, but I cut him off.

"Left!" I shouted. "Water takes the path of least resistance, and once that rain gets heavier it will create a debris flow along the burn scar, and all of it will slide onto the main road since that's where gravity will take it first. The back road on the left is longer but safer because it's a more gradual descent."

Big, fat drops started to cover the windshield as he drove as fast as we safely could down the road.

My phone buzzed three long vibrations—the sign for an emergency alert. The screen lit up with the words *Flash Flood Emergency*. I swiped the phone to open the alert and read the full text.

"What is it?" Jay asked, knowing what those long vibrations meant.

I read the alert to him. "Flash Flood Emergency. Doppler radar indicated that at least two inches of rain has already fallen across the county, with additional heavy rainfall expected. Streams and creeks are quickly filling up. Water-covered roadways have also been reported. Communities downslope of the Coltster Fire burn scar area may need to evacuate, as mudslides and debris flows are possible."

The storm had already moved through the city and was making its way directly to the burn scar location.

Jay quickly called in to his boss, giving him the bare bones of what had happened and told him to have the police meet us at the station.

His boss didn't ask questions—not yet, at least—but just agreed and hung up so we could focus on driving.

As we rounded the bend in the road, it gave us a view of down below where we had just been.

Mini rivers. Not streams. Not trickles. Rivers—full of brown, debris-filled water—raced down the hillside through the ash and scorched ground of the fire.

Neither one of us said anything. Jay gripped the wheel harder as he drove us down the rest of the gravel road, eyes locked on the main highway ahead—the one that would take us to safety.

# 24

## Jay

We made it.

Not gracefully, and not without skidding a few times on the mud-slick gravel as the rain poured down on us. But we made it.

The fire station lights flickered ahead. We pulled into the lot and quickly dashed inside, though we were still soaked by the time we arrived.

The firefighters on shift were out on an emergency call to rescue stranded drivers in the flood. The only people there were Thompson, Stetson, and two police officers, who were anxiously awaiting us when we arrived.

"Are you both okay?" Stetson asked. "Do either of you

need medical treatment before we start asking questions?"

I was fine, but I looked at Cora, who shook her head and replied that she was fine too.

We were situated in the common area just off the lobby, a broad space meant for meetings, not relaying details of attempted murder. We pulled chairs together as the adrenaline finally began to recede.

"Start from the beginning because your phone call didn't give us much to go on," Thompson said.

Cora started from when she was walking the fire scene, through the conversation with her sisters, and up to when Jade pulled the gun. From there, I was able to chime in and give my account of what happened as well.

The two officers who were there, Briggs and Landry, asked questions at times, but mostly listened as we explained in detail.

"We got a report of two people needing rescue off the national forest side of the mountain, and they match your descriptions," Officer Landry informed us.

My chest tightened. Darren and Jade hadn't gotten away.

They'd been airlifted out by helicopter after getting trapped on the mountain—cut off by rising water and unstable terrain.

They'd been trapped—not by us, and not by the law—but by the very thing they thought they could control—the fire and the burn scar. The very landscape they had manipulated had turned hostile, cutting off their escape routes one by one.

The officers exchanged looks, quietly satisfied with what they had gathered, before collecting their things and heading out.

The police left, but Cora and I stayed in the meeting room with Thompson for a bit.

Stetson exchanged a few final words with Thompson before heading out, leaving Cora and me behind in the sudden quiet of the moment.

A few moments later, Stetson had us follow him down the hall to his office, and Cora and I took a seat together on his couch.

"Can I get you both something to drink?" Stetson asked.

"Some water, please, if you don't mind," Cora asked, and I nodded in agreement.

Stetson stepped out of the room to grab the drinks.

I was happy for the private moment, even though it wouldn't last. I pulled her close to me, wrapping my arm around her waist to keep her tight against me.

When Jade had pulled that gun out, my stomach had lurched, and I swore my heart had stopped. I'd dealt with a lot of scary situations as a firefighter, but none as scary as seeing a gun pointed at Cora.

I turned my head, putting my forehead to her hair, and kissed the space just above her ear. "I think seeing that gun pointed at you took years off my life."

She relaxed into me and breathed a sigh of relief. "I

literally don't even know what to make of that whole situation. I thought Jade and I were more than just coworkers. I guess we weren't as close as I thought. I didn't even know she and Darren were a thing."

"Sweetheart, don't beat yourself up over this," I told her. "They likely didn't want you to know and were hiding it intentionally."

I kissed her cheek, breathing in her scent and feeling some irrational need to make sure she was alive and okay in my arms.

Stetson walked back into the room and handed us two bottles of water before taking a seat at his desk.

Thompson walked in a moment later, his hand brushing over his face, tired and obviously mentally burned out. "Not that we don't have enough proof now, but this does in fact confirm our suspicions of Mr. Derikson."

"Wait…" Cora's confused face turned to look at me. "You already suspected Darren?"

"He has been a person of interest for a few weeks now," Stetson told her, and I hoped she would understand why I couldn't tell her earlier.

"What? How did you know? Why didn't you tell me?" she asked me.

Thompson came to my rescue before I had a chance to respond. "Before you get upset, just like all my fire investigators, Rainer here isn't allowed to share information like this when it's related to an investigation. We suspected Derikson for a few reasons, but mostly because he slipped up at one of the BAER meetings. He knew details about the start of the fires he shouldn't have. But what we couldn't figure out was *why* he would have set them. Plus, a few of them seemed too complex to be started by one single person. Now we know why."

Cora didn't respond. She just stared at her hands—still trembling slightly—as if she were trying to remember what they felt like before today.

I reached over, took her hands in mine, and squeezed.

She looked up at me, her eyes filled with the stress of the day, and then her head fell forward, her chin touching her chest.

"I didn't know," she spoke quietly. "I didn't even see it."

"You weren't supposed to," I told her. "Motivated people are very good at hiding things. That's why they played nice when you asked for more information or shared your findings. That's why Jade smiled at you at all the meetings and hung out with you outside of work. All those things build trust."

"In cases like these, it's often easier for outsiders—someone who doesn't know them personally—to see these things," Thompson said.

"You saw it, though," Cora said to me. "You mentioned a few times that you didn't trust him."

"Sweetheart, I meant I didn't trust him around you," I explained. "That was coming from a complete caveman standpoint of me not wanting him touching or being close to my woman."

Stetson snorted next to me, and when I glanced up, it was to see a smirk on Thompson's face as well. The three of us had already had this exact conversation several weeks ago when Derikson's name was brought up.

She swallowed hard and then leaned into me. I sensed part of it was for comfort, but also for closeness. Like she needed to be anchored to me. I felt the same. Like we needed to feel the other was still there and alive.

Thompson cleared his throat. "We've got both of your official statements, so the rest is up to the police. For now —go home. Relax and get some sleep so you can adrenaline-crash at home."

"And maybe take a shower too," Stetson commented, noting the fact that we likely smelled like smoke and wet dog.

We spent the next week in a strange kind of limbo—not quite fully back to normal, but no longer in an interrogation freefall.

Cora had met with her boss, then with her weather service team, and finally with a therapist. Thompson had recommended that we both see one because, as he put it: "You don't walk away from a gunpoint situation without someone asking how you are really handling it," and he was right.

We answered question after question as nearly a dozen different people interviewed us. Cora struggled most with Jade's involvement. She fought back tears when describing Jade's determination that what she and Darren had done was the right thing.

I sat in on the final investigator meetings, the ones where we handed over files, confirmed timelines, made sure we hadn't missed anything, and officially closed the case.

Jade and Darren were both headed to prison and would remain there until their trials. They likely would have had the opportunity for bail had the fires not killed people. It also didn't help their case that they told the judge they didn't regret starting the fires—only that people had died.

Leavenworth stood at the front of the room, arms crossed, looking like he'd just won a war. I'd noticed Trent was missing from this particular wrap-up meeting, which seemed odd, but I chose to ignore it for now.

"Alright," Thompson said, his voice tired but satisfied. "If anyone thinks of anything else later, just come find me. Otherwise…that wraps up the investigation on our end."

Thompson stepped forward and joined Leavenworth at the head of the conference room.

"We have just one more thing to tackle today," he said and then looked at me. "Rainer."

I stood after being addressed, knowing this had to be about the inspector position, or at least hoping it was.

"You have completed all the necessary requirements for advancing into a fire inspector role and have worked very hard to achieve that," Leavenworth said. "We feel you would be a huge asset to one of our teams."

*Oh shit.*

I knew that meant there was a possibility that either Trent or I could be shifted to a different part of the state if we got selected, but I had hoped they would keep me local. Unfortunately, now that Jade and Darren had been caught, we didn't have nearly as many cases to investigate, so there likely wasn't a need for both Trent and me.

"Rainer, congratulations," Leavenworth said. "We'd like to offer you the role of fire inspector here in our Reno division."

*Fuck yes.*

It was an understatement to say that I was elated.

I smiled and nodded to him. "Thank you, sir. I'm honored to join the team."

"We'll have you fill out your transfer paperwork today and get you set up to start tomorrow," Thompson added.

Everything I had worked hard for had paid off, and I'd gotten the job here. I wouldn't have to leave Cora or figure out how to make long-distance work.

For the last week, I'd slept at her place every night. There was nothing wrong with mine, except it didn't feel as homey as Cora's. Her place felt like home. Plus, she had her cat, so it was easier for us to stay there.

In the beginning, I'd told her I needed to stay the night because I needed to be near her after what had happened. The truth was, I'd wanted that even before the incident with Jade and Darren—this just gave me the excuse I needed.

After I finished all my paperwork, I stopped by my place to grab enough clean clothes for a few days and then headed over to Cora's. I slept for a few hours while she worked but woke when my cell kept going off.

Groggily, I finally reached over to see what was going on. I had seventeen new texts, four missed calls, and two new voicemails—all from coworkers.

*This couldn't be good.*

I started to open some of the messages when an incoming call from Blake popped up.

I swiped to answer it. "Hey, man. I just woke up. What's goin' on?"

"They canned Trent's ass," he said, sounding thrilled.

What did he just say?

"Apparently there was an internal investigation going on because of what he'd said to Nicole, and because of that, they were watching him extra closely. Not sure how, but they found out he was the one who keyed your car."

"Son of a bitch," I muttered.

I'd suspected it was him, but there'd been no way for me to prove it.

"He came in and cleared out his locker an hour ago."

"Damn," I said. "I was wondering why he didn't show up to our meeting this morning."

"Yeah, I'm guessing he was meeting with the brass and getting his pink slip."

I didn't say anything in return. I didn't really have

words, honestly. After everything he'd pulled, it was hard for me to have any sympathy for him.

"Anyway, I'll let you go. Just wanted you to know."

"Thanks, man," I told him. "Do me a favor and let everyone else know you talked to me, so they stop calling and texting."

He laughed. "Meh... Maybe later."

I rolled my eyes, and we hung up.

I could have gone back to sleep, but Cora would be home soon, and I wanted to spend that time together.

We ended up eating takeout on her couch, watching bad movies, and having some naked fun time.

*Lots* of naked fun time.

That night, after celebrating, we lay tangled in the sheets with her head resting on my chest.

"This is nice," she mumbled, her fingers tracing lazy circles on my skin while I ran my fingers through her hair.

I hummed in agreement. "Nothing better than lying here naked with the woman I love," I told her and watched to see if my declaration registered with her.

She paused and then tilted her head up to me and stared.

Yeah, she'd heard me.

"I think half of me has loved you since high school," I told her, pulling her closer and wrapping my arms around her waist. "The other half just needed to catch up...and see you naked."

She snorted and rolled her eyes at me, but she was also smiling.

"I think I've loved part of you since high school, too," she said softly.

"The part you're referring to is my dick right?" I teased. "That's the part you loved the most—because it's the biggest."

"You're incorrigible." She swatted at me playfully, still laughing.

I loved hearing that sound.

I tightened my arm around her. "Yep, and you're stuck with me."

"I can think of worse things," she said as she rolled on top of me.

Within seconds, we were making out like teenagers before I buried myself inside her and finished the day in the best way possible.

# 25

**"Where there's smoke, there's fire
—and me cooking in the kitchen."**
*—It's science*

## Cora

*Meow.*

"Stop being impatient," I chided Frizzle. "I have to open the can of food first."

*Meow.*

"Whatever."

I had just finished setting her food in her dish when I heard a quick knock at my door, followed by the sound of a key turning in the deadbolt.

Jay had texted that he was on his way over because he wanted to see me before heading back to his place to shower and sleep.

He walked in, and I felt a smile overtake my face. I couldn't believe this man was finally mine. All those nights of dreaming about him as a teenager had turned into reality. Except reality was way better than anything I could have imagined.

"Mmmm...something smells good," he said, his eyes on me as he walked to my kitchen.

"Do you mean the cat food or the bacon on the stove?" I teased because cat food smelled gross, no matter what flavor it was.

"Neither. I think it's you."

He leaned down to kiss me, pulling me into his arms.

The kiss didn't last long before his lips trailed to my jaw, then to the spot behind my ear, and finally down my neck. I tilted my head back, giving him easier access.

"You definitely smell good," he mumbled against my skin. "You taste good, too."

"As much as I like where this is going, I need to eat and get to work," I said reluctantly. I still had to swing by the pharmacy to pick up my birth control pills—which I meant to do three days ago.

Although, feeling his lips on my neck, I wondered if I could push that errand to my lunch break and give myself a few extra minutes right now.

He sighed and kissed my forehead. "It's okay. I need to go home and shower and take a nap, anyway. It was a busy night, so I didn't get much sleep at the station."

"You should have just gone straight home, then."

Jay was working his last few shifts as a firefighter before taking on his new role full-time next week.

"I needed to see you first." His thumb brushed gently over my cheek. "Totally worth it."

"You should just move your stuff over here," I said. The words slipped out before I could stop them.

The kitchen went very, very quiet. Even the sizzling sound of bacon seemed to disappear.

He didn't answer right away. He just looked at me—not confused or even amused, just…searching.

I was suddenly hyperaware of everything, including my heart, which was beating way too fast and threatening to jump out of my chest.

"Then you can shower and nap here while I'm at work," I added, softer now and less sure.

For a split second, panic flickered and doubt set in.

*Had I crossed that line too soon?*

I knew we loved each other, but moving in together was a whole new layer. Still, when I really thought about it, I knew it was what I wanted. Hazel would have just gone for it. So would Iris. I needed to channel more of their energy.

This could be my real life. I just had to lean in.

"I mean…" I paused, trying to play it cool and casual, "Instead of bringing clothes over for a night or two, why not just bring it all over? You're hardly ever at your place except to sleep during the day. And if you're off, you sleep here with me those nights, anyway. It just makes sense."

"Is that the only reason?" he asked quietly, but his gaze was no less intense.

There it was. The real reason he paused.

I knew I could have simply said yes, made it about practicality and logic, but then I'd be lying to both of us.

"No," I admitted, making my voice stronger, even though my stomach was still doing somersaults. "I want you here all the time. To hang out, to chat about work, to handle the ups and downs together."

"You love me." It was more of a statement rather than a question.

"You know I do," I replied, watching his face light up with pure delight. "But if you're not ready, we can—"

"I'm ready," he cut in quickly, happiness radiating from him. "I just didn't want to push you. Are you sure you're ready to do this? Move in together?"

I stared at him for a brief moment and then smiled. "Yeah. I'm ready. I think I've been ready for a while. I'm looking forward to all the memories we'll make."

"Naked memories?" He wiggled his brows up and down, and I rolled my eyes.

"I meant *all* kinds of memories," I deadpanned.

"Yeah, but I know which ones are your favorites." He winked before kissing me again.

Barely pulling his face back, he stared into my eyes and whispered, "I'll pack up some stuff this weekend and move it over here then."

I smiled softly at him and then leaned up to give him a whisper of a kiss. "I love who I am with you. Who you make me want to be."

"I love who I am with you, too." He had no sooner said the words than his head jerked back and glanced over my shoulder.

A second later, I heard the sizzling sound and realized I had forgotten about the bacon.

Jay reached around to grab the pan and shifted it to one of my other burners, removing it from the heat. Upon further inspection, the bacon was more than done. Char-grilled was more like it.

"You're lucky you have a sexy firefighter here to help keep you safe." He puffed his chest out.

I laughed, turning to get us some plates. I'd already made toast and eggs, so we gathered everything up and ate at my counter.

I glanced over at him from time to time and realized I had many more of these moments to look forward to, and I couldn't wait.

# EPILOGUE

## Cora

*One Month Later*

The drive to the California coast was wonderful. Jay had even made a pitstop at what he called "our spot," where he had given me my first orgasm on our way to Morgan's wedding all those weeks ago.

This time, we were headed to Misty Ridge, the town where my sister Hazel lived. It wasn't far from Stratus Cove—where we'd lived with the O'Haras. Hazel had finally gotten the promotion at the aquarium where she worked and was moving into her new house. She was never one to directly ask for help, so I had organized it so that several of us would show up and help her move, whether she wanted us to or not.

"Knock, knock! Moving crew has arrived," I shouted into Hazel's apartment, as her door was already cracked open.

"Back here!" Iris hollered from what I assumed was the bedroom.

Jay and I walked in, and I saw Hector, Iris's now husband.

"Hey, Hector," I greeted, and he said hello and lifted his head in our direction as he stacked two boxes on top of each other.

Hazel, Hector, Iris, Jay, and I worked for the next hour loading all the boxes into a rental truck Hazel had gotten to move, and then we made our way over to her new place.

Her neighbor—an elderly man I guessed was in his seventies—met us there when we pulled up.

"Hazel, good to see ya again," the man greeted from the small front porch.

"Hi, George." Hazel smiled in reply as she turned to point at the rest of us. "These are my sisters, Iris and Cora. My brother-in-law, Hector, and my soon-to-be brother-in-law, Jay."

I smirked at the fact that my entire family still treated this engagement as a real thing, even though my sisters knew the real story.

"Pleasure to meet you all," George replied. "I'll be just down the street if you need anything."

Apparently, George had originally owned all the properties on the street, which included a total of five houses, using them as rental properties for years. It became too much work, so he'd sold them off one by one over the last two years.

They were all spread out enough to give them some sense of privacy, but close enough that you could greet your neighbors if you were in your front yard. I liked that for Hazel. She was an extrovert to the max and loved being around people.

"Do you know any of your other neighbors yet?" I asked her.

"No, but I bought a cookie cake so I can give some out to anyone who comes up to meet me," Hazel replied, a smile on her face.

Most people brought food to the new neighbor, not the other way around, but that was Hazel.

We spent the next four hours unloading all her stuff into the small Victorian ranch. It was a three-bedroom, two-bath house—way too big for her, but she said she was looking into getting a roommate. She'd picked the place because there was a small trail around back that led straight to the beach about a quarter mile down the ridge. If there was anything Hazel loved more than her job, it was collecting seashells and stuff down by the beach.

We'd only met one other neighbor so far, a woman in her early sixties named Dottie, who seemed friendly and was very excited to have "another woman on the street for a change."

We said farewell to my sisters as Jay and I hopped into his truck. We had decided to slip over to Wine Country for two nights for a mini getaway, and we needed it.

That evening, we drank wine on the hotel patio, walked some of the trails nearby, and took advantage of the hot tub to ease our sore muscles after lifting so many boxes and furniture for Hazel.

I had just climbed into bed for the night, wearing a cute little black nightie. The neckline dipped low and was covered in lace, with jersey material from the bustline down to mid-thigh, where it ended.

Jay had already been in bed, scrolling on his phone, but the moment I slid in next to him, he put his phone on the nightstand and pulled me close to him.

Jay was definitely a snuggler, and I loved it, but right now I didn't want to snuggle. I wanted to play.

I rolled over on top of him and sat up, my hips on top of his, and I slowly began to grind my pelvis back and forth over him.

His mouth split wide into a Grinch-like smile full of greed and hunger, but not the food kind.

Warm hands moved, gliding from my knees up my thighs, slowly lifting my nightie up. Once his hands reached my hips, he noticed there was nothing underneath and a low growl emerged from his chest.

He had on a pair of black boxer briefs and nothing else.

"Sweetheart, you're getting these all wet." He pushed his hips up, rubbing against me in all the best ways.

"Then we should take them off," I replied in the best sultry voice I could muster. "Let me help."

I scooted back, gripping the waistband and sliding them down over his hips and thighs as he lifted up to help.

Now that all obstacles were gone, I crawled back over to him, my gaze focused on his. I took him in my hands and stroked slowly, feeling his shaft swell in my fingers.

I leaned down and slowly licked the tip, swirling my tongue around him as he let out a quiet, raspy curse beneath me.

I worked him with my mouth, watching his desire build even higher. I hummed with excitement as my own ache grew stronger.

"Get up here and give me that mouth." His command was deep and guttural, nearly pained. "Ride me, baby, while I taste those sweet lips."

I loved his dirty mouth and the way it made me feel.

I released his dick from my mouth slowly, licking the tip one last time before climbing over him and sitting upright.

I wasted no time coming up for a kiss.

He gripped the sides of my head, holding me in place while his mouth consumed mine.

I gasped, needing to come up for air. I stared down at him for a moment, reveling in the fact that this man was mine. I lined myself up and sank down onto him.

I rode him slowly, savoring the feel of him stretching

me. I stared down at him, watching the sparkle in his eyes as he took in the sight of me on top of him.

His warm palms roamed over my hips, my waist, my ass, seeming to memorize every detail. He bucked up, thrusting into me when he felt I wasn't going fast enough.

In an instant, he had flipped me onto my back and buried himself deep inside me. He latched onto my hip with his right hand, supporting himself with his left forearm.

"As much as I love watching you bounce on top of me, I can't hold out much longer, and I need to come inside you, but first..." He paused, both in his words and his movements. "Marry me, Cora."

I couldn't help but laugh at him asking this again, but I quickly lost my smile when I saw how serious he was.

"For real this time," he said softly. "I want it all with you. The wedding. A family. Everything."

"You're not worried it's a little fast?"

"Do you love me?"

"Yes," I replied instantly without thought.

"I've been ready to marry you for weeks. I was just waiting for you to catch up." He grinned down at me, and I just shook my head at the craziness of this man.

He loved me, knew what he wanted, and had no reservations about going after it.

"Okay, I'll marry you...on one condition," I told him, giving him a wry smile.

"Yes, I will give you my cock every day for the rest of

your life," he teased, and I chuckled. "Whatever it is, the answer is yes."

"Make love to me," I told him as I shifted my hips to send him the signal to move again.

He kissed me as he began to slowly push in and out of me, each drive deeper than the last.

"Sweetheart, we've now gone a handful of times without a condom. One of these days, my excellent swimmers are gonna put a beautiful baby in you."

He was right.

Nine months later, our beautiful baby girl was born.

# AFTERWORD

Thank you for reading *Heat Advisory*.
I hope you enjoyed it.

There's a bonus scene featuring Jay & Cora.
Grab it here:

https://dl.bookfunnel.com/njxg64uzf0

Want more of the Cupid Meets Crime Scene series?
Don't worry—you don't have to wait long.
The third book in the series, ROGUE WAVE,
will be out on October 1, 2026.
Keep reading for a sneak peek...

* * *

Be sure to sign up for my newsletter at AllisonBettes.com
to stay up to date on all the latest news about my
upcoming releases.

# SNEAK PEEK AT ROGUE WAVE

## CUPID MEETS CRIME SCENE SERIES, BOOK 3

**The grumpy sheriff next door is the last man she'd ask for help—but she may not survive without him.**

Hazel O'Hara is a marine biologist by day, chaos magnet by night. She gets paid to study beach life—not to find evidence from a crime that washed up after a storm.

Hank, the town's gruff, divorced sheriff, is a decade older, emotionally unavailable, and infuriatingly hot. They shouldn't work—but when a sudden storm rolls in and things turn deadly, they're forced to rely on each other.

The question is, will they survive what's out there... and what's happening between them?

# 1



## Hazel

I'd never considered murder before. But I guess today was going to be an exception.

I'd moved in two months ago. Eight weeks and three days to be exact, and my neighbor was just as sexy, and just as big of a pain in my ass, as he was when I'd first moved in.

His name was Hank, and he was the sheriff of our town, Foggy Ridge. Our hot sheriff. I wasn't usually into guys like that, mostly because I had an authority problem. By that, I meant I didn't like people bossing me around or telling me what I could and couldn't do, and that was all Mr. Sheriff McSaltypants had been for the past eight weeks and three days.

*"You can't park there!"*

*"You can't mow your grass this early in the morning!"*

*"You can't smile!"*

Okay, so that last one didn't actually happen, but he was probably thinking it. A lot. But damn, was he sexy. Which must be the *only* reason I enjoyed needling him so much.

Now he'd stuck a ticket on my front door, letting me know I was in violation of some stupid neighborhood rule about washing my car in the street.

Technically, I *was* washing my car in the street, but that was because my driveway was really short and angled, which made it nearly impossible to wash it there. So, I'd opted for the cul-de-sac because it was large and gave me more room.

He hadn't even been home at the time, so how did he know? I'd only noticed the ticket when I'd gone to lock up my front door on my way out.

I growled. "Why is he such a curmudgeon?" I mumbled.

"I will not let him ruin my day. I will not let him ruin my day," I chanted as I walked down my front porch steps.

And it was going to be a great day, too. There had been a big storm last night, which meant the beach would be lined with a ton of great stuff that had washed ashore. This was the number one reason I'd moved here.

Though if I had known Grouchy McStubbornpants would be my neighbor, I might have thought twice about it.

I loved my place, though. It was a quiet, dead-end road with only five houses. The first part of our street was lined with trees, creating a tranquil forest of privacy. Then, Dottie's house was on the right and George's on the left. After that, it was Hank on the left and Dougie on the right, with mine tucked in between.

But the best part—and the entire reason I'd chosen to rent this house, even though it was slightly over my budget—was the trail behind my house that wound through Hank's backyard and down to Crescent Coral Beach.

There was nothing better than taking a stroll on the beach, but to do it at low tide right after a storm—perfection!

I crumpled up the paper in my hand, dropped it to the porch floor, and decided to stomp on it a few times for good measure before I disposed of it.

"What did that piece of paper ever do to you?" Dougie's voice sounded from behind me.

I watched him roll down the sidewalk in front of my house in his wheelchair, a comical grin on his face.

I took a deep breath before answering, trying to sound more pleasant than I felt. It wasn't Dougie's fault that Hank was a rude dictator.

"Let me guess... Another love letter from the sheriff?" he teased.

"Violation notice," I corrected. "For washing my car in the street."

Dougie laughed and shook his head as he wheeled his way down the sidewalk and started to come up my driveway as I threw the paper into my trash bin.

"I don't know why he hates me so much." I threw my hands up in exasperation.

"I've only known Hank for a few years now, but I can assure you he doesn't hate you." His voice was softer now.

I wasn't sure if he was doing it to keep me from murdering a sheriff, or if he was telling the truth.

"He sure has a funny way of showing it," I mumbled, but he clearly heard me.

His grin only grew wider. "I'll let you in on a little secret. He's a stickler for the rules."

I rolled my eyes. "That's not exactly a secret, Dougie."

"Not that part, no. The secret is that Hank doesn't waste time on people he doesn't notice."

"Well, I'd love to be un-noticed for a week or two."

"Want me to beat him up for you?" His grin grew a bit more mischievous, and while I knew he was just kidding, it felt nice to have at least one neighbor willing to have my back.

"Not today," I joked back. "It's a great day for finding things at the beach, and that's what I plan to do."

"Good luck, then," he said, waving before he turned his wheelchair back toward the sidewalk and headed down the street.

I made my way down the trail, sliding down the sandy hill that led to the beach. The cliffs on the south side made it feel almost private. The north entrance existed, technically, but it wasn't easy to access. It made me love this beach even more—made me feel like it was just mine. Well, and my neighbors. Though I'd never seen any of them down here.

I walked along the shore, surveying the piles of seaweed, driftwood, and even some dead fish that had washed up. I picked up a few seashells and put them in the bag I'd brought so I could take them home and clean them.

Then I spotted it. I couldn't believe my eyes at first. I was so excited I snapped a photo and sent it off to my sisters in our group text thread.

ME:

Look what I just found at the beach!

IRIS:

Umm…did you just send us a dick pic?

GALE:

Why is that dick bent weird?

ANNA:

More importantly, why is there a dick on
the beach?

ME:

OMG it's not a dick! It's a geoduck.

CORA:

I'm with the others… That looks like a
dick…and a really gross one, too.

ME:

It's NOT a dick. Google geoduck, and
you will see. Trust me.

ANNA:

I'm not googling that at work…I'll get
fired.

I glanced down at the creature. Okay, so maybe it was a little on the phallic side. But just a little.

I moved along, ignoring my sisters' weird comments,

and continued to search for goodies. I'd already found a purple snail, which was rare on the Northern California coast because our waters were usually too cold. Then I'd found two whole sand dollars, fully intact. So far, this was turning out to be a fantastic day at the beach.

As I continued to stroll along the shore, something black and sparkly caught my eye under the driftwood.

I gasped. "Ooooh…is that…a black abalone shell?"

It looked huge, but it was definitely shiny and had what appeared to be a few barnacles on it. I reached down to grab it and pulled it up.

What?

Okay, this wasn't a shell.

This was…duct tape. Wrapped around a trash bag.

*What the hell was this?*

It was shaped like a brick. It also weighed as much as a brick.

I looked down at where I had found it and spotted another. Part of the black bag on that one had been ripped off. I noticed clear plastic…with a white cake…That was when it hit me.

I'd seen these before on the news.

And heard of them washing ashore before.

*Oh God.*

I hadn't found barnacle-covered shells. I'd found bricks of drugs.

*Oh shit.*

*What did I do now?*

*Was this a 911 situation?*

Probably not. It wasn't exactly life or death.

I could call Hank, but he'd probably think I had something to do with it. Bare minimum, he'd probably write me a ticket for taking things from the beach or something.

"Ugh." I sighed.

I had to call him. Even if I looked up the non-emergency number, they'd likely just call Hank, anyway. It would be better if I did it myself.

I pulled out my phone to call him, my fingers hesitating for a few moments before finally hitting the call button.

"Sheriff McAlister," he answered gruffly.

"Umm…Hank? This is Hazel," I said nervously into the phone. "Your neighbor, Hazel. Hazel O'Hara."

"I know who you are, Hazel." His response was polite but with a tinge of annoyance.

Of course he did. He knew exactly who I was. Apparently, down to the minute I washed my car.

I'd better get this over with.

"I'm at the beach behind your house, and…well…I found drugs," I explained and then used my toe to lightly kick away some of the driftwood to reveal a few more black bricks. "And by the looks of it, I found a lot."

* * *

BUY ROGUE WAVE NOW
at www.AllisonBettes.com

# ACKNOWLEDGMENTS

Thank you to all my readers, editors, street team, betas, and friends. This book would not be possible without you.

To Jenn and Dan: Thanks for answering all of my hypothetical "what if" questions about wildfires and arson :)

Andie, Leah, Sara, Jenny, Monica, and Laura — you ladies are the best and I love you forever!

To Frauke at Croco Designs — thank you for making my books look beautiful inside and out.

To KJaspersenDesigns for designing my beautiful covers for this series.

To Sara Tonks Photography for the lovely author photo :)

To my husband...for sticking with me through all my crazy book conferences, release days, and the "research" you so lovingly offer to help with ;)

# ABOUT THE AUTHOR

Author photo by Sara Tonks.

Allison is a romantic suspense author who writes about soft-hearted badasses with brave, sassy women at their side—and she loves creating a good plot twist. She is a meteorologist/science writer by day, and a cupid-meets-crime-scene novel writer by night.

Her journey into the world of romance and suspense started when her grandma handed down her well-worn copies of Danielle Steel and Nora Roberts novels—she was hooked.

During Covid times, with time on her hands and a need for catharsis, she dove into writing her own romantic suspense novels. Her books are a thrilling blend of spicy romance, adventure, and suspense— think *Cupid Meets Crime Scene.*

www.AllisonBettes.com

facebook.com/AuthorAllisonBettes
instagram.com/authorallisonbettes
tiktok.com/@allison.bettes